D1604468

Ain't No Sunshine

Ain't No Sunshine

Carra Roe

dive bar press
n.y.c.

Ain't No Sunshine
Copyright © 2023 by Carra Roe

ISBN 979-8-9859732-1-1 (paperback)
ISBN 979-8-9859732-0-4 (hardcover)

Printed in the United States of America

First American Edition

10 9 8 7 6 5 4 3 2 1

for Charlie

Ain't No Sunshine

Chapter One

Champ placed her thumb on one side of a Granny Smith. On the other side her swollen fingers wielded a dull butter knife. "Lissen'up Bunny, next time you at the food store you needs to fill out one of them applications. Union protections come with them jobs; can't fire you none. And know why? 'Cause if they fire you it means one less vote for them union boys to sell."

"Is that so?" asked Bunny, without looking up as she filed her fingernails.

"It's true," said Champ, "When I worked there them big union bananas would roll-up and out they'd pop with some Washington, DC Fancy Pants on a string. All smiles they was, just to come shake hands with us poor folks."

"Huh; I can't say I've ever met a Washington, DC Fancy Pants, or a big union banana for that matter," said Bunny.

"You lucky; they rank."

"Rank?"

"That's right, they rank of bleach. They keep themselves a tablespoon's worth of bleach-paste hidden inside them pocket hankies. Once them big bananas climb back in them limos, they pull out them bleach-hankies and scrubba'way the poor-people-handshake-virus; believe it. Why else you think them limos got tinted windows? It's so no minimum-wagers catch'em scrubbin'off their handshakes. We a disease to them, but they need us."

Bunny blew the dust from her fingernails before sliding her emery board into a small white purse. She walked to the front door and peeked outside.

"You ignorin' me?" asked Champ.

"I'm not ignoring you, I'm just trying to gauge the temperature outside, that's all."

"So then answer me this: you want me to ask that two-legged dog next door to put in a good word for you? He's down at that food store every day, chasin' carts 'round; dirty lil' mutt he is. Just tell me, I'll do it."

Bunny smiled. "I know."

"So then speak up girl, what's it gonna be? World's waitin' on you. You needs to start chirpin'. What I always say, it's the quiet ones who get trampled on 'cause no one knows they under foot; believe it."

"Well, what about your New Year's resolution?" asked Bunny, "You said you're done with Lil' Mr. Russell, so how are you going to ask him to put in a good word for me?"

Champ gave Bunny "the look" before asking, "You just wakin'up? A Momma's job is to do what she don't wanna do. Sacrifice ain't nuthin' new; story's as old as dirt. So if it helps you any, I'll bring that lil' terrier a box of Milk-Bones. Once he smells them treats he'll do anything I ask. Just tellin'ya now though, that tongue come out his snout, I'm gone."

"Who're you kidding, you love Lil' Mr. Russell's big tongue." said Bunny, with a smile.

Champ sliced a piece of apple. "Just 'cause you older don't think wooden spoons stopped workin'. I keep'em hidden all over this house for moments like this."

Bunny grabbed Big Hank's old pea coat and put it on. Champ shook her head. "Jacket's way too big on you; you know that, right?"

"How could I not know," said Bunny, "You tell me every time I put it on?"

"So then move on from it, plus it stinks."

Bunny rolled her eyes. "What can I get you from the store?"

"When you going?" asked Champ.

"Gee, I don't know; why'd I put on this coat again?"

"Well, who knows with you; you treat that damn coat like some Linus blanket. Half the time you wearin' it to bed."

"So then, I guess you don't need anything?" asked Bunny.

"Hold on, hold on. Where's my purse at? How 'bout you pick up a coupla'them granny apples, and somathem' green olives too. Take five dollars out my purse."

"That's okay, I got it," said Bunny.

"Oh, you know what? If they got them spongy little roosters, then somathem' too."

"Spongy roosters and Granny Smiths, you got it."

"Don'tcha go forgettin' my green olives." said Champ.

Bunny rolled her eyes.

"Who you keep rollin' them eyes at?"

"I'm rolling them at you," said Bunny, "If we're playing games tonight, no green olives."

"Say who?"

"Say me. And just so you know, them spongy little roosters ain't roosters; they're little chicks called *Peeps*."

Champ sat up on the edge of the couch and looked serious. "You talkin' to a farmer's daughter, right? Right? So let this farmer's daughter teach'ya somethin'. You can't tell if they roosters or hens 'til they waddle or grow some comb, and since they ain't doin' neither, they all roosters to me."

Bunny didn't feel like arguing, she was too busy planning on forgetting Champ's green olives. And that's because Champ liked to pour the entire jar of green olives and its brine into a cereal bowl, and fish out the olives one by one. Any time the two of them played board games the dice were always wet. The lone time Bunny served Champ her olives on a napkin, Champ pretended they weren't there.

The storm door opened itself and smacked shut. "I swear the wind knows that latch's broken." Before Champ could finish her sentence the storm door opened a second time and smacked shut again, louder.

"Oh! That reminds me, know what I been meanin' to tell you, Bunny? Know how them rich gayboys from the City keep buyin'up all the mansions here in Forest Hill? They turnin'em back into single family homes, *'to showcase their original, magical splendor,'* they say. So I was thinkin', what if you go and flip yo'self a rich gayboy? They all shoppin' at the same food store as us."

Bunny looked at Champ with one eyebrow raised. "Flip a rich gayboy? They ain't pancakes."

"No, but they a happy bunch. Prob'ly treat you nice, too."

"Sorry Champ, it ain't happening."

"Lissen' to me now; you go hang 'round them endcaps and once you spot a well-groomed fella with an earring in the wrong ear, you crash into that boy, hard. Pin'em tight 'gainst the chips; them bags is loud so you'll startle'em just fine. Once you pressed-up on that boy, slip a hand into his shirt. While yo'fingers runnin' wild through that hairy chest, you look deep into his eyes and whisper, '*So what'chu think Sugabear?*'"

"*Sugabear?*" Bunny shook her head as if she were trying to shake the idea out of her head.

"Hear me now," said Champ, "Them boys ain't used to a woman's touch."

"Uhm, yeah; and there's probably a reason for it," said Bunny, as she curled the tip of an imaginary moustache, "*Ancient proverb say conversion therapy no work.*"

"Quit talkin' like a Chinaman," huffed Champ.

"It's Charlie Chan; he's Hawaiian."

"Just do what yo'Momma says."

"Do what my Momma says? I think my Momma needs to quit reading those tabloid magazines; that's what I think. You seem to think every gay man is looking for a girl to play his beard. This isn't Hollywood, this is Newark."

"See, you already talkin'off opportunity."

"So that's what you want for your daughter?" asked Bunny, "For her to marry a gay man?"

"I don't see what the big deal is. You know he's neat; prob'ly cooks, might iron, too; what's left to fight about?"

"So then what's holding you back?"

Ain't No Sunshine

"Me?" asked Champ, "I'm just an old lady. My wings already hittin' the treetops. But you, you still got time. And don'tcha feel bad 'bout havin' no interior motive; everyone's workin' an angle, believe it."

"Do you honestly believe that; that everyone's working an angle?"

"No, I know it. And know how I know? 'Cause it's common knowledge that livin' in a mansion beats cleanin' one."

Bunny reached over and pulled an apple slice from Champ's fingers, and ate it. "I'd settle for happiness over a mansion and some dirty paper," said Bunny, as she took a seat on the chair in front of the window, and swiveled from side to side.

Champ shook her head, "I was like you once; *dumb*."

"So then let me ask you something, Champ, did you 'flip' Big Hank?"

Champ's grip of the butter knife tightened. "Don'tchu never bring up yo'Daddy with no gaybirds. I got nuthin' 'gainst them boys but they ain't nuthin' like yo'Daddy."

"And how can you be so sure?"

"'Cause I know yo'Daddy. He ain't never been soft. I take that back, Christmas Day 1942, the day you was born, he was a big'ol blubberin' sissy. Held you in his big paw like you was a lil' bunny. Stared'atcha and cried all night. I cried too; but I was cryin' 'cause after squeezin' you out I still couldn't catch

7

no shut-eye. Instead I had to play lifeguard all night, worryin' yo'Daddy was gonna drown you in all them tears."

"Tears of joy I hope."

"Him? Oh yeah; he couldn't believe he had a hand in makin' somethin' so cute, all squishy you was. Now you take'way that one day and yo'Daddy was a man's man."

"Oxymoron?"

"Who you talkin' at?"

"Relax; it's an English class thing; think boneless ribs."

"Oh, so you smart now, huh?"

"Umm…"

"Don't answer."

"So is this what brought you and Big Hank together; your ability to make others feel good about themselves?"

"And what's that supposed to mean?" asked Champ.

Bunny stood up, "It means it's time for me to go."

Champ wedged the knife into the apple, "So…I guess you don't wanna hear how I met yo'Daddy?"

"You were neighbors, right?" asked Bunny, before temporarily sitting back down.

Champ used her pinkie to brush a small animal hair off her leg. "Yo'Daddy grew up 'cross the fields from me, 'bout half-way between where I lived and where the river was; same house you was born in. Always said, best damn thing to ever come outta Kentucky; believe it."

"Him or me?"

"Both y'all, but him definitely."

"Thanks."

"Thanks what? And know what's funny? Anytime I think on yo'Daddy I still smell them raw, wild tobacco leaves on 'em. Reminds me of when we first met. He was just a lil'shrimp back then, then one day he just done popped up. Livin' all alone'll do you like that; make a man outta boy real quick."

Bunny looked confused, "What do you mean living all alone?"

"Just what I said."

"So where was his Momma?"

"Gone."

"Gone? Then why'd he always say the only thing sweeter than his Momma were her fruit pies?"

"'Cause she ain't always been dead. They was close, real close. Loved her like a puppy he did. And cared for her just as much too. The polio took her by surprise, on top of the sugar. Weakened her so much she didn't have no strength left. Couldn't lift her arms none, legs neither. Her head just kinda hung there limp, chin to chest. Her tongue'd always be fallin' out and yo'Daddy'd have to go poke it back in."

"C'mon, Champ."

"Ain't kiddin', yo'Daddy was good to her. For her birthday one year he went 'round and broke off a buncha switches. Peeled'em down 'til they was soft then threaded 'em round

9

one'nother, twistin' and turnin'em like they was them long squeaky balloons clowns Indian-burn at parties; makin' lil'Dachshunds n'stuff. Then he went 'round and collected up all his dirty socks and washed every one of 'em. Once they was all clean, he slipped them socks over them woven switches and tied 'em together into a perfect circle. Rigged it, he did, to one end of a big ol' walkin' stick he found out back. Next thing he did was go into his Momma's closet and pull out one'a her old belts. Fastened that belt backwards 'round her waist 'til it was snug, then slipped-in that tall walkin' stick up her backside. Carefully lifted up his Momma's head and gently slipped it into that sock-covered crown of woven switches. Whispered in her ear she was a queen."

"Aww," said Bunny, with an exaggerated upside-down smile."

"And know what? That whole rigmarole held her head up just fine. Wheeled her out on to the porch he did, and once his Momma saw the sun break, tears done burst outta her eyes. First time in years she saw somethin' beside her own little curled hands layin' dead in her lap. That's when yo'Daddy picked her up and placed her on the porch swing. Sat there together they did, all day long 'til the sun fell down."

"Seriously? said Bunny, "I want to cry."

"Sweet he was, right? Explains how he got as strong as he was too. It was from carin' for his Momma like he did. Why yo'Daddy was an early riser too; used to say he was the rooster's rooster 'cause he'd wake-up that rooster whenever he was readyin' his Momma for the sunrise. Then come sundown he'd lift her outta that porch swing and put her back into her chair and wheel her inside. Feed her, bathe her, ready her for bed, only to wake up and do it all over again, every day."

"Every day? How old was he?"

Champ thought about it for a second, "Five."

"Five?!"

"I'm a liar, five and a half."

"How'd he even lift her?"

"Oh, she was just a skinny little thing by then, not much meat left on the bone. As I remember her, she'd always be sittin' there on that creaky porch swing, lookin' like a weepin' willow in the breeze. And yo'Daddy, he'd always be right there besides her, talkin' her ear off, little chatterbox he was. Only when he'd spot me walkin' past with my fishin' pole did he clam it."

"So wait, Daddy had eyes for you even back then?"

"Suppose we both did. Times was different; neighbors looked out for one'nother back then; at least 'til everyone found themselves a property line dispute, or somebody's Sunday paper gone missin'."

"So how'd you look after Daddy, as a neighbor?"

"For one, I used to fish 'til sundown. Did that on purpose knowin' yo'Daddy'd be back inside carin' for his Momma by the time I came walkin' past, again. Did it just so I could leave'em a catfish. I'd drop it right there in his milk box. Didn't want him feelin' funny, me leavin' him food. Knew he had no money, and no free time to fish, neither. And know what? As long as I knew yo'Daddy he ain't never once talked 'bout them catfish. He was proud yo'Daddy; wouldn't take no handouts from no one. Nuh-uh, he'd fightcha first, believe it. So I never once brought up them catfish, and neither did he."

"Wait, so how old was he when his Momma passed?"

"Already said, he was just a lil'shrimp. I reckon he was prob'ly eight or nine by the time she finally passed."

"That's so sad," said Bunny.

"Oh yeah, life's full'a sad. In them last years, his Momma'd always be asleep on that porch swing while yo'Daddy'd be inside fixin' stuff. Come one sundown yo'Daddy went out on the porch to fetch her; but like a poppy pod, she must've dried-out in the sun. Once yo'Daddy lifted her up, she done popped. Said it was like a bag'a unbleached flour had gone and exploded on him. Before he could make sense of it, wind just swept her away. She was all gone; Momma-dust."

Bunny looked terrified, "That horrible."

"Nuh-uh," said Champ, "That's love."

"Hold on; so Daddy got stuck taking care of himself since then, at eight or nine years old?"

"What other options a lil' farm boy got?"

"Well, what about his Daddy?"

Ain't No Sunshine

"What about his Daddy?" said Champ, "His Daddy was prob'ly most handsome fella in whatever boxcar he was ridin'. But to answer how we officially met, yo'Daddy came knockin'. Lucky for him I wasn't fishin' that day. Opened the screen door, I did, and there he was just standing there all fidgety and nervous. Couldn't get no words out. He reached down into his pocket and out comes a handful of somethin'. Threw it up in the air, he did, and a big'ol cloud of Creole-magic glitter come floatin' down between us, hypnotizing me some. Yo'Daddy pointed to the road, to some rickety ol'pushcart he'd been pushin'. And on the back of that pushcart was a big'ol rusty cage he done made outta his Momma's wheelchair spokes."

"Just stop right there; Daddy made a rusty cage from his Momma's wheelchair spokes?"

"Prob'ly wasn't rusty to begin with."

"How have I never heard this before?"

"You hearin' it now."

"So what was in the cage?"

"Poppin' popcorn," said Champ, "Just that it was rainbow-colored. Now it wasn't real popcorn, just looked like poppin'corn; at least to me it did."

"So what was it?"

"Yo'Daddy had himself a cageful of lil'rainbow buntings flyin'round. Catch'em wild he did, and sell'em five-cent a piece. Said they was too pretty for the wild and needed rescuin' 'cause feral cats be feastin' on 'em. Couldn't stand to watch it none."

"You know what?" said Bunny, "I bet that explains why Daddy never spoke about all those catfish you left him; the feral cats probably got'em first."

"Could be," said Champ, "They crafty, them cats."

"And so what about the rainbow buntings?"

"Whata'bout em?"

"Are they the same thing you see in pet stores, like the little lovebirds?"

"Assume so; just wild."

"So did you buy one?"

"Nope, bought two. Yo'Daddy said they needed buyin' in pairs otherwise they got no reason to sing. Just a whole bunch of Creole-magic talk that was, 'cause them lovebirds never sang nuthin'. Alls they did was mess, and lots of it too. Prob'ly went through a newspaper section a day."

"Yeah, but think of all the joy they brought you."

"Joy?" said Champ, "Only joy them poppin'corns brought was for them prowlin' tomcats, maybe. Standin' room only it was, all of 'em lined up on two legs, peekin' in my porch windows. From inside it sounded like a symphony of cat tails whippin' 'gainst the glass; all of 'em daydreamin' 'bout the hootenanny they'd be havin' if only they could get inside."

"So really," said Bunny, "The cats stalking your neighborhood weren't just tomcats, they were peeping-tom cats."

"Worse," said Champ, "They was opportunists layin' in wait. Given the chance each of 'em woulda become fate-mongers; believe it."

"Well," said Bunny, "Thankfully that wasn't the case."

"Say you; but Lord knows I'd be lyin' if I said I didn't thinka'bout accidently leavin' my door open a time or two. Always imagined them prowlin' cats be tiptoeing in. Before anyone wised up, they'd be pawin' them lovebirds right through their cage; slappin'em like tetherball. And that free paw of theirs, the one not being used to smack them lovebirds, well, you just know they'd be usin' it to fix themselves a lil' napkin bib."

"I'm not gonna lie, Champ, that's kind of morbid."

"Morbid? Ain't morbid, just shows you life's fragile. Ain't nothin' on this planet that's not a fate-monger away from becomin' a burped feather; believe it."

"Well, I'd like to believe I'm my own fate-monger."

"You think so, huh?" said Champ, with a smirk.

"I do; I own the choices I make."

Champ leaned in towards Bunny like she had a secret to share. "You can own them choices all you want, don't mean others ain't makin' plans based on the choices you done made."

Bunny swiveled away before swiveling her chair back to face Champ, "Now, why'd you have to go and say all that stuff? Now you got me feeling all sad."

"Sad?" asked Champ, "What's to be sad'bout? I said *maybe* I imagined leavin' that back door open, I didn't actually do it. My thinkin' was fate always be sneakin' into everything, right? So I imagined helpin' it along some, that's all. Ain't nuthin' to be sad'bout; them lovebirds lived it good."

"They lived it good; inside an old rusty cage?"

Champ shrugged, "Better than bein' eatin' as I see it."

"I'm not so sure," said Bunny, "It sounds like a pretty miserable existence."

"Say you."

"Regardless," said Bunny, "It wasn't your birdicide fantasies that saddened me; it's all that '*Creole-magic*' talk; it just makes me miss my Daddy."

Champ sighed, before turning the apple over to its fresh side, "You ain't the only one baby, you ain't the only one."

Chapter Two

Champ carved out a fresh slice of apple and held it up to Bunny as if it were communion. Bunny accepted the slice and placed it between her teeth while taking off Big Hank's coat. She laid the old pea coat down on the arm of the sofa, before taking a bite.

"So now what?" asked Champ, "You ain't goin' to the store no more? Where's my five dollars at?"

"Nice try," said Bunny, "But I didn't take your five dollars."

"You sure?"

"Yeah, I'm sure."

"So what's this mean, I ain't gonna have no green olives tonight, neither?"

Bunny sighed, "You and the damn green olives. It's about to pour out. Let the storm pass and then I'll go; okay?"

"Oh right; I forgot you allergic to umbrellas."

Bunny moved her head from side to side as if she were mimicking Champ talking. Champ too, moved her head back and forth, mimicking Bunny mimicking her, before they both quit and sneered at one another.

"So here you go…" said Champ, "You got five seconds to ask me any question in the world, go: 1…2…3…4…"

"Were there a lot of Creoles back there?"

"Back where? Back where you was born? You don't remember Kentucky none? Why sure there was Creoles, and before us there was more Creoles, even lotsa Creoles at one time. But once them French traders who used that bend of river, once they left, with'em gone mosta the laborers."

"Who exactly are we talking about, Champ?"

"Who, what?"

"Laborers? Are we talking about chained Creoles?"

"Not once our Lord and Savior sent them missionaries to buy-free some Creole salvation, but then *The Great Flood* came anyway, and washed everyone out; animals too. Hares got flooded right out their holes. Leapt for higher ground they did, only their higher ground was inside waitin' stew-pots. How town got its name: *Rabbit Hash*, tastiest place in all Boone County."

Bunny laughed, "Such a stupid name," she said.

Champ's head pulled back, "Stupid? Ain't stupid; nuthin' stupid 'bout it. That's where you from and don't forget it. Just 'cause you got tall here don't mean nuthin'; you ain't from here. You as Kentucky as its bluegrass, believe it."

"Well, I'm not in Kentucky anymore, am I? I'm right here in Newark, New Jersey; and I've been here more years than I've ever been in Kentucky."

"Why you wanna go'gainst me?" asked Champ, "You embarrassed of where you from? You wanna be from here, *big, tough, Brick City?*"

"Hold on, can you please use that *big, tough* voice again?"

"You needs to wake up, Bunny; ain't nuthin' here. Sun don't even shine here. And just in case you forget it, they gone ahead and planted the Statue of Liberty right where they did, just to remind you."

"Remind you how?"

"Remind you how? How you think; the whole damn state looks at where the sun don't shine on Lady Liberty. Why else you think people always be sayin' Miss Liberty *'you-know-whats'* on New Jersey?"

"Miss Liberty '*you-know-whats*' on New Jersey? Sorry, but I've never heard anyone say that."

"No? Then you got select-listenin' disease 'cause people be sayin' it. And know why they sayin' it? 'Cause it's true. One of my Bingo girls' husband works for the Parks Department. She said in three months' time when that big July 4th Bicentennial celebration comes along, and all them pretty fireworks explodin' up over Lady Liberty's head, fireworks be explodin' down below too, just no one'll see'em 'cause everyone's too busy lookin' up into the sky."

"What are you talking about?" asked Bunny.

"I'm talkin'bout how Parks pulls the cork every July 4th."

"Pulls what cork?"

"Lady Liberty's cork," said Champ, "It's the momma of all enemas; a full year's worth."

Bunny smacked the palm of her hand to her forehead, "Oh my God, Champ, it's truly what I've feared most; your brain is officially taffy."

"That ain't funny," said Champ.

"Champ, Champ, listen to me; you cannot give a statue an enema."

"Says you; but guess what, they do. Said *you-know-what* runs right down her leg and into the harbor; takes 'bout an hour or so to flush her clean."

"It's impossible," said Bunny, "And even if it were true, which it isn't, if you gave Lady Liberty an enema, everyone would smell it; and then everyone would make a big stink about it; or a bigger stink."

Champ crossed her arms in a slow, exaggerated fashion. "So tell me this then; how's it all them Independence Day tourists flock back to Dubuque, Iowa or Gumbo Flats, Mizzoura, or wherever they at, and the first thing they be tellin' friends and family is 'Holy Prosciutto, them I-talian boys sure do take the cologne thing seriously.' Well, guess what? It ain't cologne, dummy, it's sulphur; Lady Liberty's sulphur."

"See, and all this time I thought that was Staten Island," said Bunny, before smiling widely.

"Um-hmm, bad part of human nature you displayin'; can't be steppin' on things when they easy to step on."

"Staten Island?"

"Yeah;" said Champ, "Staten Island folk is good people. Ain't no different than you and I. Take'way them velour sweat suits and they 'bout normal, everyday people."

"You can't turn this around on me, Champ. You're the one stepping on New Jersey by saying it stinks."

"Hold on, alls I said is there's a scent when they give Lady Liberty her enema, that's it. Ain't no knock, we Creoles even got a name for it, *Eau de Toilette*."

"Uh-huh," said Bunny, "So explain why everyone says New Jersey is the best kept secret?"

"Best kept secret? Say who? Only secret is, ain't no gardens in a place callin' itself '*The Garden State*' even if Miss Liberty herself ready to dole out the fertilizer."

"So then why are we here, Champ? You're the one who bused us here. What; you figured, 'Hey, let's move up North and experience the '67 riots firsthand; and in its aftermath we can endure years of urban blight?'"

Champ was silent. She looked away for a moment before clearing her throat, "Urban blight, huh? You needs to give them ears a rest from that NPR; them call-ins is scripted."

"Nice try; but there's no way their call-ins are scripted."

"So naïve you is. Talk-radio, newspapers, and talk-TV, ain't nuthin' but a showcase of planted seeds to get folks worked up, to snatch some votes."

"Fair enough," said Bunny, "But how does this make the issues at hand any less relevant? The truth is, our local commerce is lean, no outside investment exists here, and to find a half-way decent job you still need to cross the river. Not to mention, where are all the local banks for our small business loans? And if you haven't noticed, there's not a single bookstore in this city. And where are all the movie theaters, or supermarkets? How many years did it take us before we got our only food store back? And who even cared other than those of us who suffered through it?"

"So what, now you all serious? Pass me the newspaper; I'll make you a paper hat."

"Whatever, Champ."

"*Whatever Champ*, what; like I'm too simple for yo'sophisticated observations? I see it; everyone sees it."

"Do you, though?"

"Of course I do. But what'chu want me to do, get all worked up so when nuthin' changes my blood pressure'll shoot thru the roof? Oh Hell no; I'm too old for that."

"That's just it, Champ; you said it; nothing ever changes. DC, Gary, Indiana and Newark; we're the only three major cities in America that have gone from a white majority to a black majority in the blink of an eye; and we're being punished for it. The people running the show here, they don't reflect us; and they probably never will. The mighty dollar and the gravy train it pulls, that's far more important than *We the People*; or should I say, We *some* People. But hey, if you're looking for a case-study in the perpetual ooze of power and city corruption, and its effect on the rise of poverty, gangs, crime, failing schools, or poisonous water, well then, I've got just the place for you."

"Hmm," said Champ, sounds like you and yo'soapbox is the ones who don't like it here."

"Soapbox? And I love it here; why else do you think I'm so vested in helping Newark rise again?"

"Vested, huh? Why sure, whatever you say; you got my vote, Mayor Bunny."

"You make a joke of it, but why not me?" asked Bunny, "The people of this city deserve someone who cares. I'm not looking to line my pockets nor am I looking to pretend I care just long enough to leapfrog my way to DC. This city is still healing and the people here need someone who'll fight for them, and not just when election season hits. Newark needs authenticity; and who better than someone who grew-up on these streets, and graduated from our schools?"

"Hallelujah;" said Champ, "But don't forget we in Newark, now; you keep chirpin' like that and someone'll dispatch a crew to kick-out yo'soapbox; among other things."

"UGH! You make me want to scream."

"Yeah, and why's that?" asked Champ.

"Because you keep throwing around 'soapbox' whenever I share an opinion; it belittles me. Not to mention it mocks everyone who speaks up for change."

"I see," said Champ, "So now you the catch-all for what the people want; like you the mouthpiece, huh?"

Bunny's eyes squeezed closed as she grimaced while rubbing her forehead. Her hand slid down her face, "Why do you think I volunteer so much?" she asked, before opening her eyes and looking at Champ. "Aside from my civic interests, and helping people, volunteering allows me to keep the temperature of our community. I know what people are saying; and trust me when I tell you, my observations are not unique; people want change."

24

Champ nodded in agreement, "Right, so by you volunteering over at the library, and checkin'-out all them harlequin novels, that's how you keepin' the temperature, right?"

"What do you do, Champ? What do you do besides criticize everyone and everything?"

"Look who's criticizing now…"

"Let me ask you something, have you ever once stopped to think about how every time you disparage Newark, or New Jersey, you're actually dumping on us?"

Champ raised both palms like it was a stick-up, "Oh mercy, I forgot you was Miss Brick City now. I'll be more careful to what I say; I promise. But let me answer the question that got you so worked up, as to why I moved us here? It's pretty simple, really. Sometimes life unfolds all by itself. Comes a time in a person's life when they realize they ain't got no control over where their magic carpet flies, they just happy when it don't crash."

"See," said Bunny, "That's an outdated way of thinking."

"What'chu know 'bout anything?" huffed Champ.

"I know you, I, and everyone have the power to change anything; ANYTHING."

"Yeah, so what'chu gonna change?" asked Champ.

"If I could change anything?"

"Like right this second; what'chu gonna change?"

25

Bunny paused for a moment, "For starters, I'd eradicate the status quo."

Champ closed both eyes before reopening them with a furled brow, "Say what?"

"Yeah, the status quo; gone. Every election season for as long as I can remember, I've been talked at like I'm some mindless, trainable, lever-puller."

"Yeah, and?"

"And that's just it; what has the status quo ever done for me or anyone in this community? All the status quo does is guarantee us that our elected officials will live in a nicer, safer, and more expensive neighborhood than our own; with a fat pension. I mean, look around."

"Where'm I lookin'?" asked Champ.

"Everywhere! Why should kids today, in 1976, have to dream about dribbling a damn basketball, leaping for a football, or becoming a slave to some music mogul; all just to make a good living? This is what year after year of dedicated vote-blocks has gotten us? White kids go on to become titans of industry; for fun they'll buy up sports teams, or start music labels. But us; well, we continue to get redlined every which way imaginable, and nobody does squat about it. But look at the bright side, now we star in McDonald's commercials, we get tapped to sing the first two verses of a racist anthem at major sporting events, and if we're really talented, polite, and keep our mouths shut, then Corporate America will reward us;

we'll get to peddle overpriced sneakers that only white kids in the suburbs can afford. I mean, really? It's so ridiculous, Champ. If this is the best my vote can do, then I'm going the other way with it; *believe it*; as you would say."

Champ placed an apple slice on her tongue, "Devil you know is better than the Devil you don't," said Champ, before crunching her slice. "And things a lot more complicated than you making them out to be. Not to mention, I think you missing a big, key ingredient in that recipe you just threw down. But tell me this; what's wrong with the Puma Clyde? It's suede."

"See Champ, it's that '*Devil you know*' nonsense; it's that propaganda that perpetuates the status quo."

"Well, I guess that means we must be at the crossroads of one of them generation-gaps, huh? Prob'ly also explains why you been gettin' fresh with me, too."

Bunny struck the floor with her foot to halt the chair from swiveling, "First off, tell me when I've ever been fresh to you? And second, if you think needing more lanes for financial opportunity is a generation-gap issue, then you just keep on doing what you're doing. But as far as my generation goes, the way we see it, unless we're entertaining white folks in some capacity, then society isn't interested in hearing from us; unless of course, it's to stand us up in front of the Viet Cong."

"Hmm, forget entertainin' them white folks; you entertainin' me right now."

"Laugh it up, Champ; but if you strip out sports, music and movies, how many non-white, multi-millionaires are there in this country? Done counting yet?"

"Huh; and here I thought dirty paper didn't move you none?"

"It doesn't."

"Well, good luck funding that Mayoral campaign of yours."

Bunny took in a deep breath and exhaled, "Let me ask you something, what transformative changes have you experienced since we've moved to Newark?"

"Transformative changes?"

"That's right; as in good changes."

Champ took a moment to think about it; "Me, personally? I'd have to say when that witch in the Ronald McDonald wig, the one with the cartoon overbite, once she retired that was a good day for me."

"Okay, aside from the Fish and Wildlife lady."

"Hang on, that ol'wretch ain't nothin' to breeze past. Any time I crossed the street and cast my line, she'd drop down out the tree like a spider. Smack me in the back, she would; with a citation. Accuse me of poachin' fish; sayin' it's 'off season.' Told her straight-up, fish don't got no seasons. Also told her, she needs to mind how she be treatin' people, otherwise her feet be gettin' warm come judgment day."

"Yeah, and how'd she take?"

"She said it's a felony to threaten an Enforcement Agent, and she'd lock me up if I gave her any more lip. Then I find out from my Bingo girls, her husband's a fishmonger; owns himself a big ol'fish store on Bloomfield Avenue. Worse part is, supposedly she lives in one of them big-ass stone mansions up there in Montclair. Ain't no wonder she don't want no one catchin' free fish; them taxes is crazy over there. So I ask you, how's that no conflict of interest, her rollin'up on everyone with a fishin' pole?"

"Sure, you have a point, I guess; but aside from the Fish and Wildlife lady retiring, is it fair to say there seems to be less and less good things happening around here? Everyone I speak with, well, they're tired of this perpetual malaise."

Champ looked at Bunny with one eye squinted, "You soundin' white."

"What? What kind of thing is that to say? All I'm saying is we deserve better; and we need change."

"So then do something."

"I plan to!"

"Well, talk is cheap, Bunny, that's what I'll say."

Bunny looked out the window before turning back to face Champ, "Imagine if you ever supported me, for anything? Most parents would encourage their kids if they wanted to try and make a difference; but you, all you have to say is 'talk is cheap.'"

"I don't see what the big deal is; it's true. But you know what it looks and sounds like to me? These failing schools must've done you just fine. Naturally, I ain't as schooled-up as you, so take this for what it's worth; but as far as this backwoods, Kentucky country-momma sees it, you needs to worry more about you, and let everyone else worry about everyone else. It's time to see things right. If somethin's tellin' you what it is without usin' its words, believe it, especially when it ain't good."

"What are you getting at?" asked Bunny.

"I'm gettin' at that you needs to keep your options open down at that food store. You meet one of them rich gayboys with the big fixer-upper and life changes. Them rich gayboys ain't forever-gay; they just ain't met the right spatula yet, believe it."

Bunny slapped-down on the wooden arm of the swivel chair, "Would you stop with that?! Seriously, I'm not a spatula. Not to mention it's insulting to them and to me. Maybe it's you who needs to pay better attention. Maybe it's you who needs to keep their options open?"

"Yeah? And what options mightchu' be talkin'bout?"

"Well, for starters you keep ignoring the obvious one."

"I'm listin'."

"I can think of one specific duplex neighbor that sure seems he'd like some Champagne d'Argent."

Champ shook her head, "I'm tryin' to make you smart and you go'head and get dumb. You needs to quit bringin' up that lil'mutt next door like you tryin' to pair us up."

Bunny unlocked the front window and cracked it open a sliver, "Well, I personally think you and Lil' Mr. Russell would make a cute couple. You know he lifts, right? I see him with his little gym bag heading down to the Y every morning."

"Yeah, well he should forget liftin' them barbells and instead invest in some lifts for them shoes; he ain't a stray hair over a munchkin. Now close that damn window; use the bathroom fan if you need some airin' out."

"Oh, would you look here," said Bunny, "Someone seems to be getting a little defensive. You do know Lil' Mr. Russell's an athlete, right? One of the cashiers at the food store told me they saw him playing handball at the Y and he wears a glove, like he's that good."

"Yeah, prob'ly from playin' handball 'gainst the curb his whole life."

"What's that even mean?"

"It means he's low-down, Bunny; I ain't interested, okay?"

"But he's a retired military man; a *Lieutenant Commander*. Sounds impressive to me."

"So then you pour his drinks. As far as I'm concerned, I don't give a hoot how fit he is, or how good he's at slappin' balls at the YMCA. And you can be damned sure I ain't impressed with no title he hammered into that dog-tag hangin'

31

off his collar. Believe me when I tell'ya, ain't no glory surroundin' yo'self with pickled men. Drunkards are drunkards 'cause the Good Lord made em' hollow to hold all the booze. Thinka'bout it, what good's a big 'ol gin bottle of a fella, if all he does is leak and pass out on the TV remote?"

"That's not very nice of you."

"What ain't?"

"You talking bad about people."

"I didn't say nuthin' bad, and nuthin' that ain't true neither. I know we all broke on the inside, just he broke more, and drunk."

"Well, a daughter of Jesus should uplift others. Pay it forward, as they say; kinda like those Catholic missionaries from back in the day, buying up Creole salvation. It's had a lasting effect, has it not?"

"For me it has," said Champ, "But upliftin' and liberatin' two different things. Plus, it's The Good Book that teaches us it's Jesus who saves, not us. All we can do is shine-a-light where savin's needed, through prayer. But tell me this, Bunny, who called here last night?"

Bunny looked confused. "Who called here last night? No one called here last night."

"No? So then why'd I hear that phone ringin' after midnight?"

"You're losing it Champ; that phone didn't ring last night."

Ain't No Sunshine

Champ sat-up on the edge of the couch, "So what'chu tellin' me, I'm demented?"

"I didn't say anything about dementia; I'm just saying that telephone didn't ring inside this house last night; that's all."

"I see; so then you held it outside yo'window just so you could say it didn't ring *inside* this house? I'm onto you, Bunny. You think you invented the game but you didn't. Take it from one wise ol' owl to one lil' bunny, no self-respectin' God-fearin' lady takes calls after midnight, period."

Bunny massaged her chin while looking up to the heavens, "But what if that late night call is because someone died?"

"Yeah, and so where they goin'? Look, alls I'm sayin' is anyone callin' a lady after midnight is screamin' three things'atcha." Champ's arm popped forward to accentuate her fingers, as she signaled each of her three points in 3D fashion:

1) They ain't callin' you 'cause they thinks you a lady.

2) Whoever their Plan A was, is now stickin' it with somebody else; explainin' why they suddenly callin' you.

3) Just 'cause you gettin' that call don't mean you Plan B neither; 'cause Plan B takes hold after Plan A, so if you gettin' that call 'round midnight, you like Plan ZZ. Moral of the story is, you needs to turn off that ringer by 10 pm."

"10 pm?" asked Bunny, "What happened to midnight?"

"Trust me, you don't never wanna be tempted come the midnight hour, so you build up cushion by turnin' ringers off at 10 pm."

"I think I'll be alright," said Bunny.

"Lissen' to yo'Momma, now. You go 'round scratchin' people's itches, you gonna be the one who ends up with the poison ivy; believe it."

"So…poison ivy only spreads after midnight?"

"You know what I'm saying, Bunny."

"Actually, it sounds like you're saying something much more subtle."

"Yeah, and what's that mean?"

"It means, it sounds like a mother is encouraging her daughter to *masturbate*."

"Don'tchu go sayin' that word in this house; you ain't amusin' none."

"It's a daughter's deduction."

"Oh right, you smart again. Well, here's the bad news, you ain't. All you gotta do is take-in one midnight caller and word spreads like California wildfire. Before you know it you got the whole neighborhood confused. Each neighbor whisperin' with the other askin' if the d'Argent's be holdin' secret AA meetings below Bunny's window?"

"Secret AA meetings?"

"That's right, 'cause word done spread and every drunkard in town with a lil' itch'll be throwin' pebbles atcha'window. So do us both a favor and next time you at the thrift store, buy yo'self a hot-water bottle, and unplug that phone by 10 pm."

"But what if it's one of them rich 'gayboys' with a mansion calling?"

"That's an exception; then pick it up."

"But a poor straight boy with a kind heart?"

"Dime a dozen; unplug it."

"You know what I can't figure out, Champ? Why'd you even bring this stuff up to me?"

"Bring up what stuff?"

"This stuff about men calling here in the middle of the night? We both know that phone doesn't ring unless it's a wrong number, a bill collector, or one of your Bingo girls looking to gossip."

"You think so, huh?"

"It's true; and if I'm being completely honest, I wish somebody'd call me after midnight. I live the life of an old cat lady just minus the cats. Drunkards where you at? Hit me up at 1-800-BUNNY; mention our *Confuse the Neighbors* promotion and you'll receive a limited-edition, silver-plated pebble for all your pebble-tossing needs. With its unique and identifying 'window-ping' you'll differentiate yourself from other drunkards. But you'll need to act fast because supplies are limited. Be one of our first ten callers and you'll be entered into a sweepstakes to win our Grand Prize: an exclusive 'fast pass' good for one complimentary 'Champagne-Tug' valid anytime Bunny's window-line backs-up, and places you outside of pebble-tossing range. *Offer void where prohibited;*

all callers must be of legal drinking age to enjoy Champagne. Offer valid to New Jersey residents only."

"See, now you talkin' disgustin', I raised you better." Champ turned the knife sideways, carving out a slice of apple. "And don'tcha get it in that head that you gonna become some hoochie-rebel without a cause. Nuh-uh, not while I'm breathin'. You wanna play Devil's toy and go trampin', you do it. Just wait 'til I'm seeded in this earth."

"Sit tight Champ; I'll fetch the spade from the shed."

"You ain't funny; shallow graves ain't for old ladies. And I'll tell you somethin' else; already I see what's gonna happen once I'm gone."

"Oh please, do tell."

"You gonna waste yo'money and a whole lotta time payin' for couch time with soft-speakin' professionals. All of 'em pretendin' they listenin' and takin' notes when really all they doin' is a New York Times crossword puzzle. And when nuthin' changes, you gonna go through a string of crossword puzzlers, each of 'em wearin' more expensive shoes than the last; and all of 'em armed with the same loaded questions designed to break you into pieces. Dr. Here's-a-Tissue will string you along up until your insurance runs dry, and then surprise, surprise, you magically healed. But not before they cast a spell over you that has you believin' yo'Momma's the root cause of a life's worth of trampin.' Somethin' I must've said or done when you was a youngin'; please. Save yo'money, unplug that phone by 10 pm and go to church; you fixed."

"You know what I've just realized Champ? All these little pearls of wisdom of yours, they're all just a remedy to combat your own saved-up fantasies."

"See, that's where you wrong, Bunny, I don't need nobody's pecker to validate me; we different that way."

"You are unbelievable!" Bunny stood up and pointed at Champ, "You have no right to say this crap to me! Never once have I brought anyone into this house; man, boy or thug. I'm probably the only person I know that's never faked a sleepover, snuck-out in the middle of the night or come home past midnight. Yet you make it sound like I got some toxic tramp gene in me. Since you're so certain this exists in me, it clearly means one thing: it's hereditary. So what's this all say about you?"

Champ lifted a slice of apple to her mouth and paused. She pointed the apple slice at Bunny, "You talkin' like you 'bout ready to sin; you know that right? Even if you Miss Innocent as you say, if someone came lookin' you'd entertain. You always been curious like that." Champ gently placed the apple slice on her back teeth and crushed it, "You knows I'm right."

The corners of Bunny's mouth sank as her eyes welled-up. She fell back onto the chair and swiveled around to face the window. Champ pressed the dull knife into the apple and slowly see-sawed it down to its core. She sensed she went too far. Champ was looking for a bridge to cross, "Bunny, why you always gotta make it seem like I'm naggin'atchu?"

Bunny ignored Champ and instead looped two big bunny ears with her shoelaces before crossing them, dipping one under the other and pulling them far apart. Bunny stood-up straight with her back to Champ, and continued looking out the window. She reached for Big Hank's old pea coat and put it on; buttoning it up to the top button.

Champ wanted to clear the air but Bunny kept her back turned. "Hey, you in the pea coat," said Champ, "There's somethin' you needs to hear from me."

Bunny reluctantly turned and faced Champ.

"You needs to remember one thing Bunny, and that's that you surrounded by love. I love you, Sweet Jesus loves you, and the Almighty Father loves you; plus yo'Daddy's watchin' over you too. You blessed."

Bunny gave Champ "the look" before asking, "So what, by you telling me I'm blessed you get a free pass to assault me?" Bunny slammed the window shut.

"Assault? What'chu know 'bout assault?" asked Champ, "You make it sound like a crime for a Momma to talk straight to her baby. I got news for ya; ain't no fun doin' the dirty work a Momma's gotta do. If it wasn't for me tellin' you everythin' you didn't need hearin', you'd be collectin' wrinkled dollar bills off the stage. I thank Sweet Jesus everyday he listened to my prayers. That's what going to church gets you, someone who'll listen to your prayers."

Bunny rolled her eyes, "As usual, I'm flattered by your expectations of me. And I appreciate you seeking divine intervention to keep me off the pole. Any mention of dirty massage parlors in your prayers, or is that still a viable career path for me?"

"Funny you ain't," said Champ, "One of these days you gonna see I prepped you just right."

A slice of apple slipped loose from Champ's knife before bouncing off her knee and falling to the floor. Bunny watched as Champ rocked back and forth on the edge of the sofa, trying to reach the fallen slice.

"Goodbye, Champ," said Bunny, without turning back, as she opened the storm door.

"Hold on," said Champ, "You tell yo'Momma you love her be'fo you walk out that door."

Bunny turned and looked back at Champ. In a breathy, sultry whisper, *"Throw a dollar bill down, and I'll tell you whatever you wanna hear, baby,"*

Champ leaned back on the sofa, "See, you overplay'n it, Bunny. And that storm door's 'bout to crack you good; wise up," but the storm door smacked shut before Champ could finish her sentence; and Bunny was gone.

Chapter Three

Bunny winced as the storm door smacked shut behind her. She knew one of these days it would slam hard enough for its big glass window to pop-out and shatter. Already it was loose and starting to rattle; not ideal for how hard the wind was whipping today.

The food store was only a few short blocks away. Bunny flipped up the collar on Big Hank's old pea coat. From one of the jacket's pockets she pulled out an old pack of Big Hank's cigarettes. Only recently she replaced his *Minton's Playhouse, Harlem, USA* matchbook from the pack's clear cellophane wrapper. In its place she slipped in her only surviving photograph of him. It was a small black and white snapshot torn free from a photo-booth strip. In the image a half-smoked Kool hung from his lips. His sailor's cap was tilted-down close to one eyebrow while his pea coat collar was flipped-up high. He posed with a slight squint as if to look hard, or to keep the cigarette smoke from burning his eyes. Based on how long his hair was, he must've been out of the service for a bit. Thinking back on his ever-changing hairstyles was a soft memory for Bunny; one that was usually interrupted by Champ's voice, and how she was always nagging Big Hank about his hair.

"You might as well smoke in the damn house 'cause this whole house stink like some damn pool hall. And what good's you always sittin' by that window blowin' yo'smoke through the screen if it blows right back'atcha? I put my face in a towel; it stink. I lay my head on a pillow; it stink. That nappy head of yours is like a dog-catcher, but fo'cigarette smoke. It's nasty, Hank, and that's why you needs to quit smokin' them fags or cut that damn wig 'cause I ain't havin' it. Bums walk-

up on me in the food store and do a lil' sniff-sniff test over my shoulder, only to then ask me if they could bum a smoke. That's an insult to a lady, and to all us who don't do cigarettes. Not to mention, it ain't safe havin' no stranger walk up on no lady like that. But you don't care, you just keep on puffin' away like you God's gift to chimneys."

"Baby, first off you ain't got to be scared none. Ain't no one messin' with Big Hank's old lady; you know that. Second, them bums is people too. They just want to meet themselves a pretty mama, that's why they doin' it. They don't really smell nothin' on you, it's just one of them classic lines men use whenever they see themselves a hot mama."

"Oh yeah? Then tell me this Hank, why's it the last man who came up on me poked me in the damn foot with one of them blind man sticks, huh? That's right, a blind man walked up on me and asked me for a damn cigarette. He ain't seein' no hot mama; he's smellin' them fags on me, all 'cause of you. Tellin' ya now, this shit's gotta change."

"Baby, you don't think blind brothers dig hot mamas too? Look here, you want your man to be cool, right? Well, you seen them ads; if you wants to be cool you gots to smoke Kool. Plus, you told me yourself it turns you hot whenever we hit them lanes and all them fancy, dressed-up mamas freeze-up and stare at you. Sound of pink bowling balls dropping everywhere; all 'cause them mamas watching you walk-in with your man. Like you the lucky one, and not them. Well, if I

43

ain't cool then no one's gonna look, right? And then you ain't the lucky one no more; is you?"

"I'll take my chances."

"Trust me, Champ; you don't wanna be married to no square. And just so you know, 'that smell' you always talkin' about, well, that smell ain't no smoke smell; it's fresh, wild mint. Them fags are specially designed to give-off a mint-scent. And you know why? Because the world's top tobacco scientists discovered wild mint is in the same wave-length family as cat-nip; just one chromosome off. Still has the same effect though, just this one affects human-kitty instead. And know how I know it's true? Because that scent even makes God-fearin' church ladies like yourself an Olympic gymnast once them lights go out. So why don't you tape-up them wrists, chalk-up them hands, hit that light, and break-out that old horse routine you so good at, with them wild swingin' legs; what'chu think?"

"Hold on, so you sayin' you smoke them fags for me?"

"For us, yeah. Plus, everything I do is for my mama."

"So then quit for yo'mama."

"I tell you what, if it's botherin' my mama that much, then I'm gonna stop."

"You mean that Hank, fo'real? You gonna quit smokin'?"

"Quit smoking? Hell no. But I'll quit growin' my pomp for you. This way less mint-scent gets trapped in my wig, then less mint-scent on them pillows, then less cat-nip effect in our

bedroom, then we both get bored, probably even uptight. And before you know it we start actin' like white folks and buying-up guns. That's what'chu want right? 'Cause if that's what'chu after, then you go right ahead and make this Kool man square. Then our cat-nip marriage go on the rocks, and before you know it, all good times be in past tenses, and I start reading gymnastic stories in the privacy of our bathroom, wonderin' where all them horse routines gone; or if they still out there, just in some other mama's gymnasium."

"Oh yeah? Well then you better chalk-up yo'own damn hands tonight."

Champ turned her back to Big Hank before reaching over and turning off the nightlight. Every ten seconds or so, she swatted away Big Hank's hand until he finally gave up and unleashed his signature "big-baby, huff-pout-bounce", a 180-degree jump-turn-away-from-her that usually sent her airborne off the mattress. And as expected, it only took about thirty seconds or so, before the whole bed started shaking like a freight train.

Champ lay there grossed-out, but was more concerned with what Big Hank planned on doing with that dirty hand of his once he finished doing what he was doing. Just then Champ felt something pat her on the head. She sprang-off the mattress and snapped-on the nightlight. She touched her hair and looked at her fingers; sticky fingers.

Carra Roe

In what seemed like slow-motion, Champ turned and faced Big Hank, seething. But the cow had already jumped the moon, and Big Hank was fast asleep after having rolled into her warm spot on the bed. To make matters worse, Champ could now see the rest of Big Hank's honey puddled-up in his hand. She quickly snatched all the pillows from the bed before he could paw one of their new pillowcases. Just then an idea came to mind, and one pillow-unzippering later, Champ was tracing Big Hank's sleeping lips with the tip of a feather. She watched in delight as Big Hank dried his big ol' honey paw against his lips, as he chased away her soft, feathery-touch.

The next day Big Hank came home after work, seemingly with amnesia. There in the kitchen sat Champ with her girlfriend Eulie, who does Champ's hair every Thursday; only today wasn't Thursday.

"Mr. Kool, come sit down," said Eulie.

Big Hank looked at Champ who nodded him to the open chair in the middle of the kitchen. Just as Big Hank sat down, Eulie reached down into her salon bag and withdrew a giant pair of sheep-shears. Within seconds Big Hank looked like a prized Blue Ribbon show lamb.

"Big Hank, we ain't never realized how pretty you was," said Eulie, as she and Champ giggled. "I think you about ready to step into the pages of one of them sweaty maintenance man calendars; the ones with them big ol'buff boys in their greasy, torn t-shirts, all holdin' their big wrench.

46

Ain't No Sunshine

What'chu think Champ; Big Hank pin-up material with this new haircut?"

Big Hank looked down at the handfuls of his hair lying on the kitchen floor. He stood up and walked over to the bathroom mirror, knowing he was being watched. Coolly he checked his profile, one cheek at a time. Without saying a word, Big Hank crossed the hallway and entered the bedroom; locking the door behind him. He closed each window before grabbing Champ's undersize vanity chair to sit on. He leaned back on the little chair and kicked-up his dirty work boots on Champ's freshly ironed, white-lace bedspread. From his shirt pocket he pulled out a fresh pack of Kools and packed them tight against his thick hand. Using just one match he chain-smoked the entire pack. To keep from getting bored, he puffed large floating rings into the room's trapped air; and with sniper-like precision he blew scores of tight, smaller rings through the large floating target; Champ's pillow being the bullseye.

As much as Bunny adored her photo-booth snapshot of Big Hank, she could only look at it sparingly; it hurt too much. She knew if Big Hank were still alive today, their lives would be different, very different; and she'd likely be very different too. If for nothing else, she imagined having more self-confidence; after all, having Big Hank around was like her having her own private fan club. He was her champion, her encourager, her protector, and her safety blanket. But now he was just her ghost, and not a very good ghost either; otherwise things wouldn't have unfolded as they had.

Bunny stepped off the school bus to find a Boone County Sheriff's car parked in their front yard. Off to the side was Champ in her nightgown, standing zombie-like, with Eulie hugging her.

Bunny sprinted towards Champ, "Champ, that ain't what I think it is, right?" asked Bunny.

"Be strong, Champ," said Eulie.

"Champ, tell me."

"Yes, baby...lockout," said Eulie.

Bunny ran up to the Boone County Sheriff tugging at his arm, "Please, no...I need to get inside. Please, I'm supposed to get a few minutes." Bunny knew from other kids at school she's supposed to have enough time to pack a bag when foreclosed upon.

"Take your hands off me. Your Momma's had plenty of time," said the Sheriff.

Bunny's panic shortened her breath. Just...for...a...sec...ond...please..." The Sheriff pulled his arm away. Bunny could feel her chances of getting inside slipping away. The Sheriff looked over at Champ to call Bunny, but Champ wasn't there; she was lost in a fog, shaking.

Bunny grabbed the Sheriff's arm for a second time. In a guttural wail of desperation she cried-out, "I just want my photo albums...please!"

The Sheriff hesitated for a second, "Okay," he said, "Let go."

Bunny let go and the Sheriff slipped inside. A moment later he re-emerged. In his hand was only Big Hank's old pea coat. He tossed the old coat at Champ's feet and quickly sealed the door. Bunny collapsed against the Sheriff, clinging to his pant leg, "Please, you don't understand...my Daddy's gone..."

The Sheriff walked towards his car with Bunny still attached; wailing as she dragged through the dirt. "Goddamn it, lady, call-off this kid." Bunny finally let go; collapsing in defeat and sobbing into the earth.

"Everyone listen'up," said the Sheriff, "I'm required by law to inform y'all you is now trespassing. If I have to come back here, Momma's goin' to County and Lil' Lady's goin' to Child Services. Do I make myself clear? Now Momma, wake up and put on that goddamn coat and make yourself decent; ain't no wonder these kids got no shot."

The following night Champ and Bunny boarded a bus for Newark, New Jersey; or as Big Hank used to call it, Brick City. For twelve hours Champ stared through a dirty bus window. Only when Bunny would nod-off did she allow herself

49

to shutter; all the while wondering what she and Bunny would do if this Lieutenant Commander Jackie Russell Jr., or whoever he was, didn't remember owing Big Hank a favor?

Bunny slid Big Hank's cigarette pack back inside his old pea coat. At the blinking-light halfway between their duplex and the food store was a thrift store. Their prices were good but some days it just felt like the whole store needed a shower. Each piece of clothing smelled like someone's sweat, or urine. On Mondays shoes were half-price but they made your feet stink like Lysol. The store divided its clothes by color instead of size which never made sense; at least not to Bunny. Champ on the other hand, she was indifferent. She didn't care how they divided their clothes because unlike Bunny, she wouldn't wear clothes that "somebody died in." Bunny knew Champ didn't always feel this way; she only became anti-thrift store after "*the crash.*"

Champ knew she had eaten way too much turkey on Thanksgiving, so to track just how much was too much, she stepped on the bathroom scale and looked down. "Not good," she mumbled, before stepping off and recalibrating the scale to zero. Just as she was about to step back on, she dropped her robe. Being semi-nude would give her a more accurate (and lighter) reading. Naturally she could still declare a deduction because traditionally, she'd only weigh herself after a successful bathroom sitting; unlike today.

The scale's reading still seemed off, so Champ decided to give it one more try; but this time she'd drop her underwear too. And so she did; and once she looked down, she gasped. Champ felt a sudden surge of uneasiness. She reached for something, anything, to help steady her. A strange sensation of lightheadedness consumed her, before violently crashing into the tub; taking down the shower curtain and rod with her.

Champ lay in a daze folded-over the tub's edge, half-in, and half-out. In the midst of her crash, the fallen curtain rod hit the hot water handle and turned on the spout. With the waterproof curtain now in the tub, it securely covered the tub's drain. And because Champ lost most of her strength over the years, she was unable to lift herself out of the tub. Her life-long fear of drowning suddenly felt like an eerie prophecy as the tub slowly filled with water.

Upstairs Bunny was flipping from Side A to Side B on her new thrift store find: an original pressing of Sun Ra and his Arkestra, on El Saturn Records. During the flip Bunny heard what sounded like faint screaming coming from next door. She knew ever since Lil' Mr. Russell's hearing worsened, his adult films became noticeably louder. And so the screaming continued, but it no longer sounded like it was next door.

51

Bunny peeked out her bedroom door and listened some more. She tip-toed downstairs and listened intently; the screams were coming from inside the bathroom. Bunny leaned down and peeked through the keyhole. She couldn't believe her eyes. Champ lay bent over the bathtub with her flower in full-blossom. Bunny scanned the bathroom to see who just put the screaming in her, but the mystery man was out of view. She did, however, notice the running water, and thought Champ was slick for using the ol' running water gag to drown-out her lady-wails.

Bunny stood up before leaning back down and peeping through the keyhole, again. While it was none of her business, she was still intent on seeing who the magic man was; a man so talented he could leave his host moaning and quivering, even after delivering the goods. Still she saw no one. Quietly, Bunny turned the door's handle and slipped her head inside. She peeked behind the door but the room was empty. Confused, she looked back towards Champ and that's when she noticed the shower rod sticking up out of the tub.

Bunny shot through the door. She tried lifting Champ out of the water but Champ was too top-heavy (or Bunny was too top-weak.) In a panic, Bunny ran next door for help, forgetting to turn-off the water.

In a flash, Lil' Mr. Russell and Bunny returned together. Lil' Mr. Russell turned-off the hot water and yanked on the waterproof curtain. It made a loud suction-noise as it separated from the drain. Lil' Mr. Russell turned to Bunny, "I just need me a quick second to catch my breath, then I'll help."

Lil' Mr. Russell used the tip of his shoe to drop the toilet lid and sat down. From his shirt pocket he pulled out a soft pack of Kools, and lit one; as his eyes stayed locked on Champ's flower. After a few quick puffs, he flicked his butt into the bathtub, and then started barking orders: "Bunny, listen up. We gonna 'clean and jerk' Champ to safety. First off, you gonna need to jump into that tub with her. Okay, good; now you gonna lift-up her shoulders just enough so you can slip underneath her. Okay, good; now I want you to treat her like a squat at the gym. Once you get her to where your legs are straightened upright, that'll have lifted up her top-half plenty. At that point all's you need to do is play defense in case she start fallin' backatcha. In the meantime, I'm gonna be doin' an 'upright row' with her bottom-half, by wrapping my arms snugly around her waist and pulling her back towards me. Rest assure, together we gonna get her out this damn tub. Now you gonna push and I'm gonna pull on the count of three, ready? One...two..."

But "three" never came; instead, Lil' Mr. Russell went to a silent count. Or if he did say "three" it was too muffled to hear because his snug grip caused him to burrow his head deep into Champ's flower. After a few quick seconds of out-of-sync push-and-pull, the two of them successfully hoisted

Champ up and out of the tub. She fell backwards and landed hard on the bathroom floor, in an upright, sitting position.

Still in a daze, Champ sounded confused. She mumbled something about feeling so close to drowning she could feel fish swimming through her. Even now as she sat there, it still felt like a fish was wiggling around inside her. Just then a pair of arms popped-up from underneath her and strapped across her thighs. Champ's eyes burst open, "AIN'T NO FISH!" she shrieked.

Lil' Mr. Russell arched his back as Champ's eyes crossed and her head rolled back; a signal that she was still dizzy, or that Lil' Mr. Russell had a big'ol dog tongue. Bunny suspected a little of both, as Champ shoed her out of the bathroom before her lady-wails chased Bunny up the stairs; forcing her to blast the volume on her new Sun-Ra record.

It took a week or so before Champ would talk to Bunny again. And that's because Champ blamed Bunny for the entire sequence of embarrassing events. It turns out the day of "the crash" Champ rose just before dawn and got dressed in the dark. She reached down into the laundry basket and grabbed a pair of freshly laundered underwear and slipped them on. Later that day when she was weighing herself, Champ removed her underwear and that's when she noticed something startling. Inside her underwear was a bold name written in black marker; it read "FANNY WOOD," aka the recently passed-away, "filthy old church lady." And that's when Champ realized in the darkness of morning, she must've accidently grabbed a pair of Bunny's thrift store underwear.

But Bunny wasn't having any of it; nor was she willing to accept any blame. She didn't ask Champ to accidently slip-on her favorite pair of second-hand underwear; nor did she ask Champ to give people mean little nicknames. If Champ didn't have a bad habit of nicknaming everyone, then the late Miss Fanny Wood wouldn't be "the filthy old church lady," and Champ wouldn't have gasped once she realized she was wearing "the filthy old church lady's" panties. It also meant Champ wouldn't have become lightheaded, nor would she have crashed into the tub, nor would she have accidentally pinned Lil' Mr. Russell's head to the bathroom floor; or have him sip her nectar. But most of all, it wouldn't have caused Bunny to bust a subwoofer on her speaker.

A short time later Champ laid down new house rules:

1) She and Bunny would have separate designated laundry days.

2) She and Bunny would have different colored laundry baskets.

3) Bunny's laundry basket would be equipped with battery operated hazard blinkers; and be blinking at all times.

Bunny didn't object to any of the new stipulations, however, she did object to finding her favorite pair of second-hand underwear cut into little snippets, and hidden beneath a large empty vinegar jug inside the bathroom's tiny trashcan. And once Bunny confronted Champ about the trashcan snippets, Champ declined comment only to say, "Trust me; I did you a favor. She was a filthy old church lady."

Bunny shook her head in disgust, as Champ too, shook her head in disgust. But Champ's disgust had more to do with the genesis of the late Miss Fanny Wood's nickname, aka "the filthy old church lady:"

One Sunday morning at church the only stall in the ladies bathroom was occupied for nearly all of morning mass. Champ couldn't help but wonder who could be so rude? Just then a pair of thick, red-rimmed, cat's-eye eyeglasses hit the floor and bounced out from under the stall. Champ recognized those eyeglasses; they belonged to Bingo Night emcee and first lady of St. Melangell's Church, Miss Fanny Wood.

Champ watched as Miss Fanny Wood's hand reached down from underneath the stall and blindly felt around on the dirty bathroom floor. Champ used the tip of her foot to nudge the eyeglasses a little farther out of reach. Just then the stall door opened and out popped Miss Fanny Wood, who quickly collected her spectacles from the bathroom floor and hurried out the door; without flushing, or washing her hands.

Champ knew there was no undoing what she just witnessed. She couldn't wait to tell the Bingo girls about Miss Fanny Wood's crimes against hygiene. In the meantime, Champ needed to be quick. If she hurried she could still receive Holy Communion despite it sounding like the procession music was winding down. For this reason, Champ didn't have the luxury of flushing away Miss Fanny Wood's "little present," and then waiting for the old toilet to slowly refill. Instead, Champ plugged her nose and did her own business, before racing out the door for Holy Communion; coincidently forgetting to flush, or wash her hands. The difference, however, is Champ added a train of toilet paper that hung from her backside like a long paper tail.

Champ jumped into the procession line and prayed others would fill-in behind her, but they didn't. She hated being last in line because it felt like the whole church had eyes on you. Even worse though, Champ knew the pew-hawks would now have an unobstructed view of her.

Led by Miss Fanny Wood, the pew-hawks were a sorority of sorts, made-up of the elder stateswomen of St. Melangell's Church. Ceremoniously, the pew-hawks occupied the first few rows at every mass and paid meticulous attention to how much wine everyone sipped during Holy Communion. Parishioners slow to hand back the wine goblets were suspected of being "compromised."

In fact, just one week earlier, at the urging of Miss Fanny Wood (and the pew-hawks,) Champ's Bingo girls staged a Bingo Night intervention, and accused Champ of being a "Cathaholic" (a wine abuser at mass.)

Carra Roe

Champ denied their allegation and was insistent her slow draw at Holy Communion was not out of need, or to catch a buzz; rather, it was her way of unlocking the small communion wafer from the roof of her mouth, without using her fingers. But because of the recent drama, and her being last in line, she decided to forgo today's symbolic offering of drinking Christ's blood; in order to loosen her communion wafer.

As the procession line winded-down, Champ was just about at the altar when the music stopped playing. The Monsignor unexpectedly turned his back and walked away. Stepping forward in his place was today's Eucharistic Minister, Miss Fanny Wood.

"Body of Christ?" asked Miss Fanny Wood.

Champ's knees buckled and her chin began to quiver. All she could think about was Miss Fanny Wood's dirty, bathroom-floor fingers holding her wafer; and no wine chaser.

Miss Fanny Wood held the communion wafer high up in the air; so high that the entire congregation was now focused on Champ's wafer. "Body of Christ?" asked Miss Fanny Wood, a second time, louder.

Champ knew if she refused the sacrament with everyone watching, she'd be the talk of Bingo Night. Everyone would speculate wildly on what her big sin was; and how she had fallen from a state of grace. Damned either way, Champ said "Amen," and reluctantly opened her mouth a sliver, as tears streamed from her clenched eyes. Just then the elderly Miss Fanny Wood inadvertently dropped the communion wafer, and instead delivered two dirty, bathroom-floor fingers; and pressed them firmly against Champ's tongue.

With no communion wafer stuck to the roof of her mouth, a confused Champ opened her eyes and spotted the fallen wafer. With a quick, windmill-like sweeping motion, Miss Fanny Wood scooped the fallen wafer off the floor and dunked it deep into Champ's mouth, before dragging her dirty, bathroom-floor fingers slowly across Champ's tongue; a second time.

Champ's gag-reflex kicked-in and her throat started making horribly strange and loud noises. If the congregation's eyes were not on her before, they certainly were now. And with each gag reflex, Champ's head involuntarily thrust forward as if she were about to throw-up. This action repeated itself over and over until a small child could be heard saying, "Mommy, look, she thinks she's a rooster."

Mortified, Champ dropped to one knee, crossed herself, and scooted into a random pew. Except to enter the pew she had to first nudge a parishioner to slide over. But the unsuspecting parishioner she nudged was praying; and Champ's nudge sent a fragile, elderly woman spiraling awkwardly off her kneeler, causing the old woman's head to "thump" the pew in front, before the old woman crumbled to the floor, concussed.

Carra Roe

Nearby onlookers gasped as the old woman on the floor clutched at her shoulder, while moaning something that sounded like a Hail Mary, in Polish. The Monsignor rose from the Presider's Chair and walked towards them. With each step, the old woman's moans grew louder and louder, as her wailing Hail Mary was captured by the Monsignor's lapel mic, and amplified throughout the church.

In a panic, Champ reached down and placed a hand over the old woman's mouth to muffle her amplified groans; except the old woman in distress bit her hand twice, in rapid succession, without letting go. "Mother Fletcher!" yelled Champ, as pain radiated up her arm. With her free hand, Champ reached down and plugged the old woman's nose, and squeezed it tight while twisting it upside down. The old woman relented; semi-relaxing her jaws, and allowing Champ to withdraw her throbbing hand; just as nearby onlookers began to catch their breath, from repeated gasps. Meanwhile, the Monsignor peeked over the pew at the old woman on the floor, writhing in pain. "Jesus Christ!" he said, while shaking his head disapprovingly at Champ; before laying his decorative stole over the old woman's protruding collarbone.

Champ dropped to her knees and began praying; praying she could please disappear; all the while her tongue worked feverishly to unlock her carpet-fuzz-covered wafer from the roof of her mouth. And while Champ knew it to be selfish to ask personal favors during prayer, she asked the Good Lord to

Ain't No Sunshine

please let there be a day when parishioners would be saved; saved from receiving Holy Communion from the hands of "a filthy old church lady."

Bunny knew if you carefully navigated the kids' aisle at the thrift store without slipping on one of the thousands of toys and picture books haphazardly strewn about, there were treasures to be had in the far back. Huddled in countless milk crates were stacks upon stacks of old vinyl records. It became an annual ritual for Bunny to go record-diving on Big Hank's birthday. She'd sift through hundreds if not thousands of records, until she found the perfect album she imagined Big Hank would have liked. Deep-down she knew this practice irritated Champ. In fact, on more than one occasion, Bunny accused Champ of trying to re-write Big Hank's musical taste, especially whenever she brought home a new jazz record on his birthday.

"Yo'Daddy was a country boy and he loved himself some country-blues."

"YOU like country-blues," said Bunny, "Daddy liked jazz."

"You don't know what'chu talkin'bout. Yo'Daddy loved DeFord Bailey; said he wanted a harmonica fo'years 'cause o'him."

"So are you saying Daddy didn't like jazz?"

"I'm sayin' you wastin' yo'money buying them dumb jazz records."

"Uh-huh; thought so, 'cause we both know Daddy loved jazz."

"Oh, you think so, huh?"

"I know so," said Bunny, "Remember that Easter Sunday when you and Daddy got into it? It was all because he wouldn't walk you to church in the rain. He had the car keys in hand while he and I stood by the front door waiting for you; all while you stood in front of the mirror fussing with your big Easter bonnet. Then you decided at the last minute we should all walk to church in the rain, instead of drive, just so Daddy could hold an umbrella high above your head; just so all the parishioners driving by would notice your new big dumb hat."

"You don't know nuthin'bout what'chu talkin'bout."

"I remember all of it, Champ. Daddy said Easter Sunday was no day for being vain; so you snapped back, 'Then maybe you should stay home.' So he did. And then you made me walk you to church in the rain, and hold your umbrella high above your head, so everyone driving by would see your new big dumb hat. And all that rainwater that rolled off your umbrella rolled right on to me. And once we got into church, no one

was looking at your new big dumb hat; instead they were fixated on me and my soaking wet, see-through yellow dress. And naturally you started yelling at me because of it. And us being in the vestibule, your yells echoed throughout the church, so whoever didn't know my dress was see-through certainly did now; and yes, everyone turned around and looked."

"Yeah they did; 'cause you wasn't wearin' no bra."

"Because you hadn't bought me one yet!'

"You coulda asked."

"Uh-huh; so is this why the Child Protective Services lady got up out of her pew and accused you of dressing me in lingerie? And when she asked me my name and our home address, you nearly yanked-off my arm and pulled me outside. Next thing I know we're running home in the pouring rain through random backyards, all to evade the CPS lady trailing us in her car. But that didn't bother you nearly as much as you not being able to receive Holy Communion on Easter Sunday; which really meant you couldn't parade-around in front of the entire congregation, in your new big dumb hat."

"Some memory you got, Bunny."

"I remember it all, including how that day went from bad to worse once you climbed up on that doghouse to help you jump a chain-link fence. The only problem was the sleeping dog inside that doghouse wasn't having any of it. So when his jaws caught your dress as you leapt, you ended-up suspended *in mid-air on the other side of that fence. And there you were, a life-size marionette puppet; and as that old dog with your dress in its mouth kept backing-up and then sliding forward, you bobbed up and down like a yo-yo, until finally that old dog's teeth gave out and you splashed into a mud puddle. Only then did you realize the entire Easter brunch gathering at the Elks lodge was watching you from inside their buffet room's back bay window."*

"You enjoyin' this, right?"

"Oh but wait; even after all of that, it got worse. Once we got home and opened the front door, there Daddy was, sprawled out in his underwear with a burning cigarette in the ashtray, listening to Sarah Vaughan records; who by the way, is filed under 'Jazz' in record stores. And not only was he listening to Sarah Vaughan records, but he had all her album covers propped-up everywhere; the ones with big headshots of her on the cover. And him being the center of some adoring, makeshift shrine, all while 'adjusting' himself, well, that was too much for you; you ran into your bedroom crying."

"You sure is good, Bunny; good at spinnin'up tales masquerading as memories."

"Sorry, Champ, but I remember it like it was yesterday."

"Right; well let me give you a dose of reality you seem to be missin'. When we walked into the house after church that day, I put my Easter bonnet on the living room chair. I told yo'Daddy he better extinguish that damn cigarette and I went

to the bedroom to get my hat box. Next thing I know, I hear a 'pop.' Knew right then the dumbass he was, he'd gone ahead and sat on my new hat. That's why I locked myself in the bedroom and cried; all 'cause it took me weeks to save-up for that damn hat, and like everything else in my life, it goes and gets ruined. So maybe now's a good time for you to acknowledge that memory bank of yours ain't no Fort Knox; like the truth has gone ahead and escaped the premises."

"So then tell me this, Champ, if Daddy didn't like jazz like you say he didn't, then why'd he have all those Sarah Vaughan album covers gawking at him in his underwear?"

"'Cause yo'Daddy was demented; that's why. What'chu gotta understand is men ain't made right; always fantasizin'bout what they can't have; thinkin'bout what was, or dreamin' of what coulda been, instead of ownin' up to what is."

"So that was Daddy?"

"That was yo'Daddy; sorry to break the news. Ain't talkin' smack 'cause I love 'em with alls I got; just that he wasn't no saint, not by a longshot."

"I don't believe you," said Bunny.

"So don't believe me; but I got news for ya, you don't know everything."

"So what else don't I know?"

65

"What else don't you know? How'bout what do you know? Did you know 'Sassy' was a childhood friend of that lil'mutt next door, right here in Brick City?"

"Who's Sassy?"

"Oh, so I guess you don't know everythin', huh? 'Sassy' is 'the Divine One,' Miss Sarah Vaughan, aka the album cover observer of yo'Daddy adjustin' himself. And how it affect you, or me really, can better be understood with why he was actin' like a dumbass that day."

"So why was he?"

"You was too young to remember, but anytime it was fleet week in New York City, yo'Daddy's boat be docked over at one of them piers across the river. He'd go get loose in the big city with that lil'mutt next door. And naturally that lil'mutt next door bein' the hanger-on he was, he was takin' yo'Daddy to wherever his childhood friend 'Sassy' was scattin'. It wasn't 'til years later, after we came up here to Newark, that I had to pop that lil'mutt in his lip, so he'd quit tellin' everyone 'Oh, Sassy was high on 'Big Country;' her pet name for Big Hank, on account she didn't know no country boys.'"

"Is that true?"

"What'chu mean 'is it true?' You think I'm gonna get to lyin' 'bout my man gettin' with another woman? You needs to lay off that reefer, Bunny."

"I'm just saying I've never heard that before, that's all."

Ain't No Sunshine

"Well there's a lot you ain't heard. The three of 'em, yo'Daddy, that lil'mutt next door, and 'Sassy' all be out together painting the town red. Regulars they was at just about every hush-hush, secret-knock-on-the-door, back-alley speakeasy up in Harlem. Meanwhiles, I'm stuck down in Rabbit Hash, workin' my tail off to pay the damn bills, and raise you."

"C'mon, Champ. You have to admit serving our country in a time of war is stressful. Daddy's ship could've been sunk at any time, so of course whenever there was a weekend pass, they're gonna whoop it up a little. Do you really care if they stayed out late and enjoyed themselves a little of what Harlem has to offer? I mean, so what?"

"Oh, so what, huh? Well here's another lil' tidbit you don't know'bout from when yo'Daddy was overseas. Early one mornin' rooster's cockin' so loud it lifts me to my feet. I shuffle out the bedroom to make me some coffee and what I see? A vagrant done broke-in. Stealin' he ain't; instead, he passed out on the couch, right after he mugged himself a zoot suit gangster. So tip-toe I did to the kitchen, and grabbed me the heaviest stew pot I could find. White-knuckled that pot on both sides and lifted it high in the air. Justa 'bout to smash that vagrant to smithereens when the sleepy burglar pops-open an eye and screams. Scared a Snickers outta me, it did; so I scream back, which woke you, and you scream, then we all screamin'. Long story short, buried underneath that bum's

*raggedy beard and moustache is yo'Daddy; which made no
sense considerin' he supposed to be across the Atlantic
shootin' down warplanes or somethin'. What else don't make
no sense is Navy boys supposed to keep it clean and tight, and
yo'Daddy come home lookin' like he some Uptown pimp by
way of skid row. And if you still can't picture it, I'll just tell
you this: his wig was so outta wack I found a baby blue
robin's egg in it; ain't even kiddin'."*

"Nuh-uh," said Bunny.

*"Oh yeah, turns out yo'Daddy had gotten himself
discharged from the service for beatin' down the boys on his
ship. The brass got to wonderin' if he was a secret agent for
the Risin' Sun, tryin' to sabotage ship morale. But nope, just
Big Hank thinkin' he was the heavyweight champ. So
instead'a him comin' home to Rabbit Hash, yo'Daddy decided
he gonna buy himself a zoot suit and some fancy hat with a
cock feather, and secretly do himself a round or two up in
Harlem, on the sly. Rents himself a rowhouse, he does, up in
Sugar Hill. The Big Cheese he pretendin' to be goes'bout
spendin' all his prize fight money, too. Then what'chu know,
soon as them moths start flyin'outta his pockets he washes-up
in Rabbit Hash; busted and broke with a damn robin's egg in
his wig."*

*"So no wonder you don't like jazz; it reminds you of
Daddy's time up in Harlem. You're jealous of Sassy."*

Ain't No Sunshine

"Jealous? Jealous of what? What I can tell you is this: yo'Daddy thought she was so 'Divine' and that little terrier next door did too, but here's the thick'n'thin of it as I see it: anyone who answers to the name 'Sassy' is probably some damn tramp. Now, maybe that's the scorn in me talkin' 'cause truth is I actually hear she good and decent, and I'll admit she got some talent too, when she's scattin'. But when yo'Daddy chooses to rub his indiscretions in my face, whether they real or wishful, I don't care; I ain't no second fiddler; believe it."

"So that's why you wooden-spooned him out the door on Easter Sunday, in just his boxers? And here I always thought it was because he was smoking in the house."

"He's lucky that's all I did. The day our Lord and Savior resurrected, he wanna skip church, smoke cigarettes in the damn house, lissen' to jazz records, and milk himself in front of 'Sassy' record covers? Nuh-uh, not in my house."

"Can we please go easy on the 'milking' imagery?"

"You the one who wanted to talk 'bout this stuff; I'm just settin' the record straight."

"So wait, me playing jazz records offends you because it reminds you of Daddy loose up in Harlem. And the bad mood that puts you in spills over so then you start talking to me like I'm some tramp; which is really a deflection of your own pain. It's your way of making you feel better about yourself because at least you're no tramp. Now add in, if not for me, then you too could've been up in Harlem having a great time, but

instead you were stuck down in Rabbit Hash; working, paying the bills, and caring for me. And years later, when Daddy's still fantasizing about the fun times he had without you, that's unbearable for you."

"Tell you what, Bunny, now you sound'n like I dropped you on yo'head when you was a baby. Not once neither, but like I was Curly Neal and you was some Spaulding basketball."

"I'm just saying it kinda feels like the pain from your old wounds targets me, in passive-aggressive ways."

"Right, so now you Dr. Bunny, huh? Well, I think maybe it's time for you to go lay down on your own damn couch."

"I'm not ashamed Champ; I buy into the power of therapy; kind of like the church is for you. However a person chooses to massage their mind, well, God bless. We all benefit from people being happier. And that's why I can't quit jazz. Old jazz records are my therapy. Something about listening to jazz rescues me; especially listening to jazz in the rain. I'm guessing it has a lot to do with reminding me of Daddy; or maybe it's that rainy Easter Sunday from long ago; I don't know. But I'm sorry it triggers you like it does. Daddy wasn't perfect, but he adored you, and us. I think it's important for you to remember nobody's perfect Champ, not even you."

"So ain't you cute; not only you turnin' this on me, but now you some life coach too, huh?"

"I'm just saying there are no crimes in family; only hurt feelings. And now that I have a better understanding of things,

Ain't No Sunshine

I'll make some changes. While I won't be giving up jazz, out of respect for you I'll play my records at a lower volume."

"Oh, that's big of you, Bunny. Thank you. Yo'Daddy prob'ly didn't pass on no selfish gene to you; nuh-uh. But you know what, you go'head and play them jazz records; play'em loud too. Might even sound better in your own damn apartment, ever thinka'that?"

"Seriously?"

"You just do what'chu gotta do, Bunny. What's it matter how I feel? I'll block it out like I do everythin' else. What's one mo'thing to be numb'bout? It's a Momma's job; wife's too. Used to it by now. So enjoy yo'music; ain't lookin' to infringe none. But just 'cause we talkin'bout it, know what kinda music maybe I'd like to hear? It's them tunes that go somethin' like, 'Hey, Champ, can I pay the electric bill this month? Hey, Champ, can I cook fo'us, this once? Hey, Champ, let me do the dishes tonight,' or 'I'll take out the garbage, Champ.' All that'd be music to my ears; not some 'Sassy' boo-shit you got cracklin' on that dumbass record player."

71

Chapter Four

Bunny crossed the intersection and carefully walked through the parking lot of the food store. The curb had crumbled away so cars could enter and exit wherever they pleased. There were no painted lines, or arrows for traffic flow. The action in the parking lot was reminiscent of a bustling, third-world country where people, cars, motorbikes and oxen all converged; with horns honking and everyone navigating around one another, all while going in a million different directions. The only difference being abandoned shopping carts in place of the oxen.

"Geesh," muttered Bunny, as a car nearly nipped her from behind.

"Well hello there Miss Bunny, how you doing today? And how's Champ doing?" asked Lil' Mr. Russell.

"Hey, Mr. Russell, I'm good, and Champ's doing well too; thanks for asking. How are you doing?"

"I could complain; but who would listen?"

"Ain't that the truth," said Bunny, before smiling.

"The way I see it, there's no point in getting too caught-up in things. Don't know if I'm cursed or blessed by it, but fighting in a war teaches you one thing: life is fluid. Any day I put my boots on is a good day. For this reason I'll find something to smile about. Plus, it sure beats the alternative; know what I'm saying?"

"Amen." said Bunny.

"But because you asked I will say this, grocery store parking lots ain't what they used to be. Nowadays it's downright dangerous out here. I'll be pushing a train of shopping carts and folks'll speed-up on me. I even went to management and asked them to phase-out the red shopping carts; them carts have a charging-bull effect on some."

"So really, you're a parking lot matador," said Bunny, "You need a cape."

Ain't No Sunshine

"You ain't kidding; been saying it for years. Truth is, colors trigger people. Don't know why we as civilized people need to remind each other God gave man the capacity to act like savages; doesn't mean we need to use it. People need to pump them brakes. We're all brothers in arms; it's that simple."

"Well, look on the bright side, Mr. Russell, being a parking lot matador keeps you on your toes, right?"

"I guess that's one way of looking at it. Some days I think I'm only here for entertainment purposes; like little do I know I'm whistling through a tigers' cage or something. Once them cats get fixing to pounce, it'll be lights out for Jackie Russell Jr."

"Well, we are just across the river from Zoo York."

"Oh, I know it. And so you know, everything they say about them New York drivers is true; trust me."

"So why don't you just quit?" asked Bunny, "You don't need the money."

"Thankfully I don't; and that's a good thing 'cause minimum wage don't do much other than feed them unions, that then feeds their politicians, who'll use it to feed their re-election campaigns, to then feed power and privilege back to their quid pro quo cronies; 'cause Lord knows it sure don't feed the folks stuck earning it. But listen to me now, now I'm complaining. This is what happens when you get old; you start paying attention to things."

"You're precious Mr. Russell."

"Precious? Been called lots of things but can't say precious is one of 'em."

*   *   *

A man of many monikers, Lil' Mr. Russell is properly Jackland Russell Jr. He's 'the lil'mutt next door' to Champ, and *Jackie* to himself. He's also a retired Lieutenant Commander in the US Navy, and was Big Hank's closest friend in the service. He serves as Champ and Bunny's post-Rabbit Hash savior, their current landlord, and duplex neighbor in Brick City. He also holds the title for Bunny's favorite storyteller of Big Hank tales. And while Bunny knows all the stories by now, she still enjoys hearing Lil' Mr. Russell re-tell them. One story that stands out from the others took a little getting used to at first, but now it's Bunny's favorite:

"When the town doctor was filling out your birth registration after you was born, Doctor says 'y'all might use a couple extra days to think if you really wanna name this here baby 'Bunny' or maybe y'all consider 'Bunny' for a middle name; and give this baby a proper name for when she all grown up.'

Ain't No Sunshine

So the Doctor leaves Champ and Big Hank your birth registration and shows 'em where to write-in whatever name they decide on for you. Doctor tells them they have until the end of the week to mail it off to the County Clerk. So after a few days Champ and Big Hank decide they'll still call you 'Bunny' but it'd be your middle name. For your first name, they decided to go with something more proper, as the Doctor prescribed.

So Champ and Big Hank kick around a whole bunch of proper names and narrow it down to Georgia and Virginia. Now Big Hank liked Georgia because it sounded 'peachy' but Champ preferred Virginia; and that's because there's long been a rumor that Virginia is for lovers. Her thinking was, anytime she or Big Hank looked at you, you being Virginia, well, you'd remind them of their love for one another; and the love that created you.

So come end of the week, Big Hank had to hurry to town, to mail-off your birth registration 'cause the Post Office closed early on Saturdays. Don't sound like no big deal except for one thing: he and Champ never 'officially' came to an agreement on what your proper name would be; and Champ was still snoozing that Saturday morning.

Now everyone knows Champ sleeps like a bear in winter so Big Hank gave her a good nudge. Champ responded by cracking one eye and growling like a Montana grizzly. Now Big Hank ain't never been stupid so he heed that warning real

77

quick and instead took it upon himself to get things done; and that's just what he did. Plus, he liked the idea of telling Champ he wrote-in his preferred name of 'Georgia' even though he'd secretly write-in 'Virginia' just as Champ's been pushing for. Big Hank figured once your birth certificate came in the mail, he'd let Champ open it and she'd be shocked and overcome with joy, knowing she really got her wish, you being Virginia, instead of Georgia. And considering Big Hank's birthday was just around the corner, he hoped maybe all that joy and celebration would spillover too, for some extra-special birthday celebrating, Big Hank style.

So days pass and one afternoon Big Hank comes home to find the County Clerk's envelope in the mailbox. So Big Hank hides the letter for about a week, and on his birthday morning he lays the envelope out on the kitchen table for Champ to find. Sure enough Champ wakes up, sees it, rips it open and screams. She screams so loud the catfish jump out the crick.

Now Champ's got tears pourin' out her eyes and Big Hank circles 'round and comes up from behind. He wraps his big meat hooks 'round her and delivers a soft, delicate, little ear kiss. Champ turns and faces Big Hank, but her joy looks more like unbridled rage. In what Big Hank described as 'a hissing-like warning by way of forked serpent's tongue' Champ erupts: 'Get yo' hands off me; and dontchu NEVER touch me again!'

Ain't No Sunshine

Now you know Big Hank, he ain't never been scared of nothing. But once he heard the Devil's voice come outta Champ, he scooped you up out your bassinet like you was a fumbled football, and ran you back to the bedroom and locked the door behind him. He said Champ had gone possessed and he couldn't figure out why. So while rockin' you in his arms he yelled through the door askin' Champ why's she so hot? He hears nothing back but silence. So Big Hank puts his ear up to the door and listens. Just then a butcher's knife blasts through the space beneath the door, and stabs the sole of his black Chucks. Champ pulls the knife out his sole and then sweeps the space beneath the door; back and forth, back and forth, until finally her forearm wears out.

Big Hank waits a few minutes and asks again, why's she so hot? Champ responds the same way, with silence. Just then a small piece of paper slips underneath the door. It's your birth certificate. 'Read it!' says Champ. 'Read it out loud so I can hear you.' Now, Big Hank thinks it's just a ploy to stab his hand, so he busts-up a hanger real quick and uses it as a fish hook to catch your birth certificate, and reels it in.

'READ IT!!!' screams Champ; louder and angrier than before. Big Hank glances down and reads it aloud: 'Virginia Bunny d'Argent,' he says. With that Champ grabs the door handle and shakes it so violently it breaks in two. Big Hank looks down and sees Champ's eyeball staring up at him from where the door handle used to be. It spooks him so bad he

79

tucks you extra tight into his cradling arm and climbs out the bedroom window. The two of you escape into the fields and hide there all day and all night of Big Hank's birthday; all while Champ's running through them tobacco leaves, banging her wooden spoon against a stew pot, yelling she's gonna make rabbit hash out of Big Hank, once she catches him.

Now what you gotta keep in mind is this: everyone knows Big Hank's strong enough to pull a small tree out the ground but one thing he ain't; and he'd be the first to tell'ya; he ain't no Scrabble champion. And that's 'cause Big Hank had gone ahead and skipped years of schooling to take care of his Momma.

See, after his Momma passed, Big Hank did go back to school; but what he quickly realized was whenever his classmates got called on to read, they all sounded like Shakespearean actors. Sure, they were reading Hamlet, but still, Big Hank was the only one using a finger against the page. So kids being kids, well, they ain't too shy 'bout chuckling; at least not 'til they get shushed by the teacher. So Big Hank knew right then he was in for a rough ride. Problem was, all them little hyenas was too small for Big Hank to whoop. He figured even if he rearranged all the desks for a Battle Royale, where he'd take on the entire class at once, he knew the next day he'd have to do the same for all their pa's; and whoop them, too.

Ain't No Sunshine

So Big Hank says, screw them little jackals; him being as handy as he was, he figured he'd quit the classroom and instead start fixing things, for money. And so he did; and his choice to do so explains two things: one, how Big Hank became the master maintenance man he was; and two, how Kentucky's Boone County Clerk knows you officially proper as Vagina Bunny d'Argent.

Now, Big Hank said on account of Champ being a woman of her word, he had no interest in becoming rabbit hash. So like most anyone else would do, he gone ahead and enlisted in the service. And he picked the Navy over the others because he knew Champ was deathly afraid of water; and he didn't want to keep looking over his shoulder for Champ and her big stew pot. He figured by the time he'd return from serving, Champ would have cooled down some; hopefully.

So the next day Big Hank drops you off with some friend named Eulie, who'd bring you home to Champ, and he goes and reports for duty. Uncle Sam busses him out to Camp Smalls, and after some quick training, they ship him off to the USS Mason. As fate would have it, that's where I first had the pleasure of meeting your Daddy, my bunky, and soon-to-be best mate, the one and only Big Hank d'Argent."

"Mr. Russell, maybe you'd like to join us for dinner tonight?" asked Bunny.

Lil' Mr. Russell's head snapped sideways, "Come again?" he asked.

"Would you like to join Champ and I for dinner, tonight?"

"Naw...really? You serious? You want me to join you ladies for dinner?"

"Why is that so hard to believe?" asked Bunny, "I think it'd be nice, don't you?"

"Well of course I do, but the truth is I don't think Champ would like it all too much. I don't want to go spoiling her holiday, or nothin'. She ain't been talkin' to me much of late."

"Mr. Russell, please stop. I'm taking this as a yes, that you'll be joining us, tonight."

"To be completely honest with you, Bunny, there ain't nothing I'd rather be doing than spending time with Creole royalty, the two of you being the queens you is."

Bunny found delight in Lil' Mr. Russell's reply; plus it felt good to invite him over considering his social interactions had dwindled down to aggressive parking lot drivers, and a much-too-loud television set. Now, normally Bunny would check with Champ first, but because she already knew Champ would put-up a big stink, she figured she'd just spring it on her, instead. Plus, Bunny thought Lil' Mr. Russell spent enough time in Champ's doghouse, after all, New Year's Eve was more than three months ago.

Ain't No Sunshine

"Ladies, look what Jackie's got for you tonight!"

"Don't tell me you brought some of that damn cough syrup again. I ain't in the mood to look at no green tongue tonight."

"C'mon now, Champ; this ain't no cough syrup. This here's a 'Godly' drink; made by monks in some secret monastery somewhere."

"Godly drink? God awful maybe," said Champ.

Lil' Mr. Russell smiled before his laugh turned to a cough and he suddenly looked like he needed to spit. Whenever Lil' Mr. Russell laughed, or coughed for that matter, his tongue popped out and unfurled over his bottom teeth. And because of this, Champ could see his laugh-cough loosened-up an old cherrystone clam that must've gone down the wrong pipe one time or another. Champ looked away while handing him a napkin. Lil' Mr. Russell promptly deposited his lung-clam into the napkin, before crumpling it up and casually dropping it under the table.

"What do you say, Champ; how 'bout a little taste of some of this here, monk-made magic sauce?"

"That's alright; I know how much you love it; you drink it."

"I do love it; and that's why I'm already one bottle in. It's New Year's Eve; Jackie's celebrating tonight!"

Carra Roe

Lil' Mr. Russell poured Champ a small helping of green Chartreuse and pushed it in front of her, before Champ promptly pushed the glass back towards him.

"Now, look here, Champ," said Lil' Mr. Russell, "I know how much you love that Kentucky bourbon, but this here green Chartreuse, well, this ain't so bad. So why not just sink one with me before the big ball drops; for fun's sake?"

Champ's eyes lit-up. She was mortified. She thought to herself Big Hank was lucky he passed-on already, because she'd kill him right about now. And that's because Big Hank had a bad habit of telling everyone about their private affairs. And how she knew this to be true is because aside from having wine at church, Champ consumed alcohol only once; and it was a jug of Kentucky bourbon on Big Hank's birthday, back when they were just teenagers. And because Champ had no experience with the potency of Kentucky bourbon, the train was already on the wrong track by the time the room started spinning. Needless to say, Champ was not her usual lady-self that evening. And ever since that night, the only thing Big Hank ever wanted on his birthdays was for them to celebrate with another jug of Kentucky "backdoor bourbon."

Lil' Mr. Russell polished off his glass of green Chartreuse and stood up. He excused himself before stumbling three steps to the left, then three steps to the right. Champ watched him zigzag towards the bathroom before turning to Bunny, "Every time that little hound dog drinks, he starts staring at me like I'm some ham bone; you watch."

Bunny laughed, "He ain't staring at you; that's just his slow-eye getting slower from all the alcohol."

Champ wasn't buying it. "Oh yeah? Then explain why that lil'mutt and all his drool looks damn near ready to flood the joint?"

"What are you talking about?" asked Bunny.

"I'm talkin'bout him salivating for yo'Momma; that's what I'm talkin'bout. Anytime you nice to a man they get deranged. They think just 'cause you ain't rude, you must be open to 'em climbin' up on you. No thanks. What men don't know is God invented us claustrophobia to keep them hound dogs off."

"Who are you kidding, Champ, you love the idea of being Lil' Mr. Russell's ham bone."

"Tellin'ya now, keep gettin' fresh and I'll bust a wooden spoon over that elbow; believe it."

"Yeah, but think about that big, fat, meaty tongue of his; and all that panting and slippery drool. Oh Lordy, you better start fanning yourself."

"Bunny, you 'bout as funny as a submarine with a screen door; already I've given too much leash to that lil'mutt. It's killin' me to sit here and play nice. Lil'fool sittin' there slow-eyin' me all night; and hiccuppin'. I'm damn near ready to punch them hiccups right outta him; ain't even kiddin'. It's annoying as all Hell.'"

Carra Roe

Bunny grabbed the small glass of green Chartreuse from in front of Champ, and drank it. She slammed the glass down and yelled, "Mr. Russell, you better hurry back; Champ wants you to pour her another glass of green monk-magic; quick, before the big ball drops."

Champ gave Bunny "the look" before exploding out of her seat.

"What; what is it?" asked Bunny.

"Bathroom's empty. He's stealing." Champ sprinted for her bedroom before skidding abruptly. She turned back to Bunny, and SHREIKED!

Bunny ran to Champ's side, who was now pointing at her bedroom. Inside the bedroom stood Lil' Mr. Russell with dropped trousers; mumbling to himself, all the while trying to put-out an imaginary fire on Champ's plastic ficas tree.

"Mr. Russell!" yelled Bunny. Her voice startled him, causing him to shuffle backwards. With his ankles cuffed by his pants, BOOM! The backs of his knees crashed into the edge of Champ's footboard, dropping him backwards on to her bed. Champ and Bunny ran down the hallway and poked their heads into the bedroom. Lil' Mr. Russell was out cold; except his penis looked like an unmanned firehose, wildly spraying green Chartreuse in every direction.

Champ stood up in disbelief, "That lil'mutt sniffed-out my tree. How you sniff-out a plastic tree?" She poked her head back inside, and gasped. Her once-white lace bedspread now looked like a green tie-dye. Champ turned and ran for the hall closet, "Bunny, where them thrift store towels at?"

"DON'T TOUCH MY TOWELS!" yelled Bunny.

"It ain't gonna stain none; they green already. C'mon now, just one; you ain't gonna miss it none."

Bunny chased after Champ who was rummaging through the towels. "Champ, no! I'm serious; use your own towels."

"I just threw-out all my damn rags; all but one. You really gonna make this old lady walk all the way down them basement stairs just to fetch that one rag; with all these thrift store towels right here? I'll buy you another; I promise."

"Nuh-uh." Bunny wasn't budging.

"You rotten, you know that?" said Champ, before heading to the basement."

"Wait, Champ; I'll get it," but Bunny never moved. Instead she listened intently. As soon as she heard the sound of Champ's foot hitting the basement stairs, she tip-toed back into the bedroom. Bunny stood by the side of Champ's bed and stared at Lil' Mr. Russell's privates; it was much fatter than she imagined. She reached down and squeezed it; twice.

"I hear you, Bunny," yelled Champ from the basement, "You best get outta there."

Bunny tip-toed back to the living room and poured herself a tall glass of green Chartreuse, and sank it; just in time for the big ball to drop.

The sound of a fender-bender in the far reaches of the parking lot caught their attention. Lil' Mr. Russell turned to Bunny, "Just someone takin' their frustrations out on another red shopping cart. It'll unlock from their bumper in the next quarter-mile, or so. Ain't no thing; I'll track it down on my way home."

"So then, what do you say, Mr. Russell, seven-ish sound okay for dinner, tonight?"

"Nineteen hundred hours it is," he said, "And you tell Champ not to worry; I won't bring any green Chartreuse this time."

"Bring two bottles," said Bunny, with a devilish smile and a wink; before turning and heading inside the food store.

Lil' Mr. Russell snickered. He already knew he wouldn't dare bring over another bottle of green Chartreuse. Instead he planned on surprising Champ with a jug of Kentucky's best *backdoor bourbon*.

Chapter Five

Walking towards the fruits and vegetables aisle, Bunny imagined Champ's response once she informs her of tonight's dinner guest: *"What?! Nuh-uh. That broken down little heathen, he ain't comin' in here, no siree. My room still stinks 'cause of that lil'mutt. For all I know he left flea eggs in my bed; just too damn cold for'em to hatch yet. Tell'n ya now, he dare come through that door he better be wearin' a diaper, 'cause I swear to Sweet Jesus I'm chainin' that little fool to the table leg."*

Bunny unfastened the top few buttons on Big Hank's old pea coat. She thought to herself how dreamy it'd be if she could just grab a few green apples from the display pyramid of polished Granny Smiths, but of course, Champ wouldn't eat those. *"Only shoes and cars for polishin'*," she'd say.

The unpolished Granny Smiths were kept inside a wooden crate beneath the display pyramid. But because the display table's skirt drooped all the way to the floor, Bunny had to reach underneath it, and feel around for firm Granny Smiths without being able to see them. The last time she reached underneath the skirt and squeezed an apple, it squeaked. It turns out the apple was a hurt sparrow. The produce manager apologized, noting they usually prefer the grapes.

Bunny looked at the big clock on the wall and wondered if she had enough time to make an old Creole favorite for dinner tonight, *Ragout de Lapin*. She had two concerns; the first being she'd still have to walk to the butcher because this store never had lapin, and second, it was Good Friday, and the butcher might not be working today.

Now, Bunny knew Champ believed if you ate meat on Friday during Lent you were going to Hell. If you ate meat on Good Friday, well, you'd probably meet the Devil himself in common hours. But Bunny also knew if you counted the forty days of Lent from Ash Wednesday, but didn't skip each

Sunday like you were supposed to, then Lent actually ends six days before Easter. So in a roundabout way, it was *maybe-okay* to eat meat today. She figured once Champ smelled the lapin cooking, she'd look the other way on her Creole-magic arithmetic.

"Two onions, a green bell pepper, a red bell pepper and okra. Two onions, a green bell pepper, a red bell pepper and okra." Bunny kept repeating the needed ingredients under her breath. She paused to scan the misty section of the vegetables aisle: celery...carrots...radish...turnips...TURNIPS. The word "turnips" triggered a flashbulb-like memory:

"You must be Little Miss Bunny! Welcome to the beautiful Garden State of New Jersey. I am Lieutenant Commander Jackland Russell Jr., but you can call me Jackie. He extended a hand out to Bunny, but she offered only a half-smile in return, before turning away, while clinging to Champ's arm.

Bunny peeked back at Lil' Mr. Russell when he wasn't looking. She wondered how someone with such an important sounding title could only be a few inches taller than her. She noticed the white hat under his arm; and fixated on the fancy scrambled eggs design on its brim. Her attention quickly turned to the gold star on his cuff; she wanted one, too.

"Mrs. Champagne d'Argent, the pleasure is truly mine. I've heard so much about you. It is with great delight that I finally get to put your face with all them Big Hank stories. And I have to say, you are even prettier than I ever imagined. And that's no easy feat on account of Big Hank always having said you was the prettiest thing in all of Kentucky. So welcome, welcome my friends; welcome to beautiful Newark, New Jersey; the only urban oasis in America where the Hackensack and Passaic Rivers converge."

Lil' Mr. Russell took Champ's hand and bowed to her; except his bow was awkward and looked more like a curtsy. Champ forced herself to smile despite really wanting to cry. She couldn't help but wonder what she was getting herself into. She believed anytime a man other than a relative complimented a lady's appearance, he was just looking to ground some corn.

Lil' Mr. Russell turned back to Bunny, "And just so you know, Little Miss Bunny, your Daddy used to talk about you ALL the time. Let's see, I know you was named after the prettiest state in all of America." Bunny quickly deflated; she figured if Lil' Mr. Russell knew she was named after a state, then he probably knew the other part, too.

Lil' Mr. Russell turned towards Champ as they exited the bus terminal, "I just bought me a duplex nearby. I live on one side, the other side is vacant. You two welcome to nest there on the vacant side as long as you want. Don't need to pay me nothing; maybe in time you just throw me a bone."

Champ's eyebrows lifted, "Throw you a bone?"

Lil' Mr. Russell placed his hand on Champ's back, and rubbed it a little, "Once you up and on your feet, maybe you just chip in for some of the taxes a little, that's all. Ain't gonna charge you no rent."

"Oh, okay," said Champ, relieved.

"Mortgage ain't too much; I can handle it," he said, "But remember now, it ain't no Taj Mahal, but it's okay. We got us Branch Brook Park just across the street. It's a beautiful park designed by the same boys who dreamed up Central Park, and Prospect Park, too. Come springtime it's lined with cherry blossoms; makes DC look silly in comparison. Come nighttime it's desolate and quiet; like rest in peaceful quiet. 'Round the corner we got us a grocery store and a Salvation Army, too. It's a real nice community; a best kept secret kinda place; except the cat's out the bag 'cause now we got us an influx of Gothamites crossing the river. How'bout this, let's grab us a gypsy cab and you can check it out. If you like it, you welcome to stay; if not, no hard feelings. I'll help you and Little Miss Bunny find a place wherever you two most comfortable at; how's that sound?"

Champ was gracious, "Okay...thank you."

As for Bunny, she was excited. This would be her first time inside a gypsy cab; or any cab for that matter. It certainly

93

didn't look like any of the taxi cabs on TV, but that hardly mattered; Lil' Mr. Russell had her full attention:

"And just so you know Little Miss Bunny, your Daddy was one tough cookie. Like he was so tough it hurt just being friends with him. He'd play around and hitcha; and when he'd hitcha, oh' Lord, he'd hitcha good; like your bones would cry out for you to go and make friends with someone else."

Bunny was eating it up; she loved how dramatic Lil' Mr. Russell was, "And your Daddy's hands were MASSIVE. They were as big as cinder blocks, only harder. And his knuckles, oh Lord, he had knuckles. It was like his hands had gone ahead and swallowed frozen turnips; that's how big and hard his knuckles were."

Bunny half-smiled at the turnips before grabbing a few vegetables while juggling the Granny Smiths. Onions…check, green bell pepper…check, okra…check, red bell pepper…none. The space for the red bell peppers was empty except for an out of place bouquet of fresh, wild mint. Bunny picked up the tiny bouquet and held it close to her nose before gently placing it on the turnips, and exiting the produce aisle.

In the check-out line Bunny surveyed the room. She always heard about people's lives changing on account of the people they meet while grocery shopping, but she was still waiting.

Ain't No Sunshine

"Patrick Daniel Charles! Put it back, NOW," said the woman in the check-out line. If some kids were a handful, this little fellow would have exhausted an octopus. Bunny watched Patrick Daniel Charles go to work. First the cherry cough drops. Next the tiny wax bottles of cola, then packets of Pop Rocks, and finally the Pez space gun. Bunny wondered just how deep the pockets were in his little raincoat. While his mother continued emptying her shopping cart, Patrick Daniel Charles was emptying the candy racks.

Patrick Daniel Charles reached down to the lower level beneath his mother's cart and covertly withdrew two trays of Peeps he'd been stashing there. "Damn!" thought Bunny, she forgot to grab Champ's Peeps.

Bunny glanced over her shoulder to where the Peeps were, and noticed the long line that had formed behind her. She was torn about exiting and reentering the long line, and ultimately decided against it on the basis of time; or lack thereof. And so Champ's green olives wouldn't be the only thing not making it home today.

Patrick Daniel Charles was at a standstill. There was absolutely no way his Peeps trays were going to fit into his raincoat's pockets. In stealth mode, Patrick Daniel Charles carefully, and quietly, slid the Peeps trays behind his mother's tall paper towels on the conveyor. Without looking up, his mother slapped his hand, as she dug through her purse searching for her checkbook. The cashier placed the two trays of Peeps on the side, along with the day's other discards: baseball cards, a yo-yo, two Cadbury eggs, a press-on moustache, and Camel cigarettes.

Relieved, Bunny reached over to the discards and politely grabbed the two trays of Peeps. In doing so, she noticed the store's last red bell pepper neatly nestled-in at the tail end of Patrick Daniel Charles' mother's groceries. Bunny looked over at Patrick Daniel Charles' mother, who was still digging through her pocketbook. Using the tip of the Peeps trays, Bunny rolled the lone red bell pepper back towards her own vegetables, and then placed the Peeps trays down as a divider.

Patrick Daniel Charles observed the heist. He looked-up at Bunny wide-eyed and in disbelief, before smiling. Bunny smiled back, and winked. A second later, Patrick Daniel Charles' mom grabbed his little arm and dragged him away while scolding him. Patrick Daniel Charles looked over his shoulder at Bunny; and flashed her one of her Peeps trays, and winked.

The cashier called-out for a price-check on okra. As they waited, Bunny stood silently while looking through the store's tall glass windows. The wind outside picked-up noticeably. The store's tall windows sounded like they were bending. "Winds of change upon us," said the cashier.

"Indeed," said Bunny, "Looks like they all up on Lil' Mr. Russell." On the other side of the windows Lil' Mr. Russell pushed a train of carts into the wind. His lead cart was unruly and bucking, seemingly trying to pull-a-wheelie in the face of a sudden wind gust.

Bunny didn't feel too bad for Lil' Mr. Russell; she knew he survived worse whoopings than the one the wind was putting on him, today. She knew this thanks to Champ having once re-enacted a phone call she received from Big Hank long ago, shortly after he boarded the USS Mason. Champ pretended her hands were phone receivers, switching back and forth between hands based on who was supposed to be talking. Champ was good at imitating Big Hank:

"So I'm lying there right, and my bunky pops his head down and introduces himself. Says he's Jackie Russell Jr. from Brick City; a personal friend of The Divine One; Miss Sarah Vaughan. So Jackie Russell Jr. asks me my name, where I'm from and a whole interview's worth of questions; one of 'em being why I enlisted in the Navy?

So I confided in him, told him all about my little spelling error, and all the troubles it brought me. He told me it wasn't so uncommon; that people make spelling errors every day. But next thing I know, every sailor on the Mason knows about me and my spelling error; each of 'em saying dumb stuff to me, trying to be cute and clever, like I'm some big dumb joke from the tobacco fields of Kentucky. Whole bunch of Tom Foolery it was, so I figured, heck, time to show-out; this Creole boy ain't nobody's chump. So once a day, after mess hall, I called out a new funny boy. Soon as they pushed Mr. Funny Bones forward, I opened a fresh can of Kentucky whoop-ass, and served it up, country-style. And with each passing day, a different boy from the laugh-now, cry-later crew, well, they each wore themselves a fresh shade of Big Hank eyeshadow; compliments of I-ain't-yo'chump. So I worked my way down the list; and when it came to my last can of whoop-ass, as in my special reserve of private stock, well, I set that can aside for one very special occasion: Jackie Russell Jr., of Brick City.

So I waited, and waited, and wanted Jackie Russell Jr. to think he was in the clear. In the meantime I find out the little serpent was getting rich off me; laying odds and taking bets on all my tussles, and didn't count me in on nothing. So that night once everyone was asleep, I clutched that little moccasin by his gullet. Grabbed him so tight he went crossed-eye. Carried him out on deck using just one hand; his little feet dangling like he was doing the soft-shoe. Hoisted that pipsqueak up like he was a bale of hay, and just before I tossed him into the Atlantic, slippery little thing squirmed out my hand and started screaming like a newborn."

"That's when I interrupted Big Hank and say 'Henri d'Argent, is you crazy?!!! You gonna kill this man? They'll string you up.' He ignored me and kept rattlin' off his craziness."

Ain't No Sunshine

"Nah, get this Champ; so he rambled a mile a minute trying to save his slippery little hide, 'Oh I didn't think it was funny Big Hank, I swear. I gotta similar story; my name is Jackie Russell Jr., but my birth name is Jackland Russell Jr. See, my Daddy and me both named after my Granny. Her name was Jacqueline and 'cause my Daddy didn't have no daddy, and my Granny bein' scorned and all, she'd always be goin'round town saying: 'Why should only men get to have juniors; after all, half of 'em casting bad spells on these boys by branding them with philandering names. So come Hell or high water, I'm gonna have me my own junior.'

Sure enough, my Daddy bein' the first born, he was destined to become Granny's junior. But my Daddy showed up late; like fourteen pounds, seven ounces late; and breech. Naturally, Granny was on the morphine drip after pushing him through, so when the doctor filled out my Daddy's birth card, he couldn't figure out what the hell Granny was slurring. So he interpreted her morphine mumbles as "Jackland" instead of "Jacqueline" and thank God he did; otherwise me and my Daddy'd be stuck in some Nashville honkytonk singin' 'bout our names.'"

"Finally Big Hank took a breath, so I asked him, "So what'chu do?"

Big Hank say, "I asked him straight-up; how much money you make off me?"

Carra Roe

"So I said to Big Hank, 'How much he say?' And Big Hank say 'He said $406.50.' So I said to Big Hank 'WHAT?!!!' and Big Hank say 'That's what I said too!' So Big Hank say to me, "I get paid $19.50 a month minus $5.00 for life insurance and $1.50 for laundry. So that leaves me $12. So after doing the math, I was about to throw Jackie Russell Jr. back into the seaweeds; but then I got to thinking, maybe he could be my manager; set up my tussles and handle the purse. So I proposed it, said '80-20 split and all losses paid out your take.' Then he come back and say '50-50 and we split losses.' So I didn't say nothing, instead I looked at him real, real hard, until he looked away. That's when I grabbed his slippery little head and pointed it seaward, 'Fine,' he screamed, '80-20 you, but we split losses.'

So I figured, heck, ain't gonna lose me none so wasn't no sticking point, so I agreed. Then I told him he also buys me a carton of fags every time we anchor AND he owes me a favor for life; considering I just saved his. Then I said real politely, 'Oh, and one last thing, Jacqueline, you tell anyone else 'bout my spelling error and some giant sea clam gonna find itself a brand new little black pearl, you dig?'"

Big Hank howled. So I waited for his big dumb laugh to end and then I said, "So where that $406.50 at Hank, I got bills to pay?" Phone line got real quiet, then it sounded like a soft fingertip gently pressed down on the disconnect; all while I'm stuck with nuthin' but my echo; 'Hank?...Hank?...Hank?'"

Chapter Six

Bunny transferred her bag of groceries to one arm while using her free hand to button-up the top buttons on Big Hank's old pea coat.

"Sorry, Ma'am, it'll just be a minute," said a store maintenance man, "We got us a safety hazard here. Automatic doors just locked up; doesn't seem to want to let you out. Got it to where it'll kind of open, but it's opening and closing way too fast; apt to close right on you. Give me a sec to see if I can figure this thing out, otherwise I'll have to take you through the emergency exit; but fair warning, that door's alarm is no joke; it'll wake you up good."

Bunny started to feel anxious, and trapped. Timing was everything today; if she didn't hurry she'd miss the butcher. She studied the door's timing sequence and leapt forward.

"NO!" yelled the maintenance man.

The doors closed catching Bunny's foot, snapping off her sneaker.

The doors opened. "Are you crazy, lady?" asked the maintenance man.

The doors closed.

The doors opened. "You got a death wish?"

The doors closed.

The doors opened. "These doors'll crush you."

The doors closed.

The doors opened. "My sneaker…"

The doors closed.

The doors opened. "Please, I'm in a hurry."

The doors closed.

The doors opened. "Thank you."

The doors closed.

The doors opened. "Wise up, lady."

The doors closed.

Bunny tried slipping-on her sneaker using just one hand before hopping unsteadily on one foot, causing her purse strap to slide off her shoulder. Her small white purse crashed to the pavement and everything in it spilled out like confetti. She stuffed everything back in, before depositing the small purse into her grocery bag. She wiggled her foot back into her sneaker and took a deep breath.

Bunny scanned the parking lot for Lil' Mr. Russell. She spotted him in the far corner and gave him a quick wave goodbye, but he missed it. Lil' Mr. Russell was preoccupied with trying to corral a runaway cart before a sudden gust of wind sailed it across the street on a ghost-ride.

The food store's doors kept opening and smacking shut, louder and faster than before. "Thank God," thought Bunny; thank God she took the chance when she did, otherwise she'd still be caged-up. The sound of loud music caught her attention. It was coming from the house across the street where "the white-boy stoners" lived. Bunny knew them to be recent NJIT dropouts with baby dreads, "finding their way" with *maybe* slightly less financial support than usual from Daddy Wall Street. At least that was the general vibe in the neighborhood; in part because these boys were forced to slum it by driving last year's models of BMWs, with surf racks on top. Bunny also knew the only time these boys pushed QPs of their skunk weed was at the end of the month when rent was due, and their monthly allowances were likely already spent.

Through a cracked sliver in the white-boy stoners' "take-out" window, a skinny cloud of pot smoke squeezed through;

along with a hefty dose of the trippy jazz piano intro for *Riders on the Storm; a* "doors" coincidence of sorts, one occurring behind her, and now one playing before her.

SCREECHING BREAKS halted Bunny dead in her tracks. Startled, she turned sideways and was face to face with her reflection, in the flat windshield of an old milk van. She couldn't help but notice the smell of burnt rubber, and the smoke rising from the van's skidded tires. Bunny took one step backwards as the old milk van jerked into gear and passed, as the driver lifted his fist and yelled something in Spanish.

"Oh my," mumbled Bunny, "Close one."

If Bunny hurried she could still drop-off her groceries and make it to the butcher. As she passed the thrift store she noticed someone just left a donation at its front door. It was an old wooden television set with long skinny legs; only someone gutted its glass tube. In its place were fluffy cat pillows. Bunny couldn't help but wonder if this was the former cathouse of *"The Sour and The Sweet,"* a missing cat duo belonging to two Chelsea chefs renovating a nearby mansion. It was Champ that suspected the cats' disappearances could be traced back to the least likely of all suspects; one of the cats' owners. Champ figured whichever of the "gayboys" was more jealous of "kitty attention" probably left the backdoor open, inviting fate to come sneaking in, or out.

Ain't No Sunshine

The unexpected cathouse donation triggered one of Bunny's earliest eavesdropping memories:

"Champ, you know them Navy boys most hated in all the armed services, right?" asked Eulie.

Champ laughed, "You don't know what'chu talkin'bout Eulie; America loves them Navy boys."

"Ain't talkin'bout America, Champ, I'm talkin'bout other soldier boys. See, sailor boys come into port for just one, two days at a time; all while their ships be refueling. Soon as them battleships drop anchor, Navy boys off and runnin' for them cathouses. So when local house-momma spots a boy in a dixie cup, prices sky-rocket 'cause house-momma knows sailor boys 'bout ready to flood the joint. And her thinking is, sailor boys don't spend no money out at sea, so they ain't never gettin' no change back; meanin' they ain't never got no coin; just bills. And naturally, you push a ship full'a boys out to sea, they get so horned-up, by the time they step foot on dry land, they willin' to pay anything to get themselves a lil'taste. Another words, them Navy boys happy to splurge and drop a crisp dollar bill on what usually costs just ten cents. After all, there ain't no ten cent bills, and cathouses don't give no change. Only problem is, sailor boy generosity don't sit well with them

Army boys stationed overseas; the ones used to paying a purdy lil'dime to get butter on that noodle."

"How you know this, Eulie?"

"Know what, the going rate? I only know the going rate for ports in Algiers and the Azores; supposedly them the big fueling ports where superstition is a religion."

"How you mean; a religion?" asked Champ.

"Well, according to local legend, unless Navy boys drop their lil' anchors in them cathouses, then bad luck's gonna find its way back on to their ships."

"Say who?" asked Champ.

"It's the thousand year old Legend of House-Momma," said Eulie, "Supposedly them house-mommas is more than a greeter and a talent manager; they also maritime historians that dabble in the Dark Arts."

"Dark Arts; as in what, voodoo?"

"As in, quit questionin' foreign customs, Champ. Point is, anytime a battleship goes refueling, cathouse girls gettin' refueled too; just with seamen semen; and no I ain't stuttering. From what I hear, ports in Algiers and the Azores make Bangkok look like Notre Dame du Lac."

Champ crossed her arms while tapping her foot steadily against the linoleum floor, "Who told you all this?"

Eulie looked at Champ like she was dumb, "How you not know this stuff; every red-blooded American knows full-well, Navy boys are inflationary."

Ain't No Sunshine

"Inflationary?" asked Champ.

"Is there an echo in here? Yeah, inflationary. C'mon now, Champ. Don't you remember that famous General Whoever-he-was? He delivered that graduation speech to all them cadets; it was on just about every movie house's news reel for a year or so. Anyways, he told them new graduates if they take nothing else from their time at the academy, they should at least remember one thing: in order to battle inflation in the years to come, it's 'fiscally prudent' to punch a sailor. And naturally him delivering that speech at West Point, well, all them cadets went bonkers and threw their caps up in the air."

"Well, I ain't never seen that; nor heard it."

"C'mon, Champ."

"I ain't kiddin'; don't even make no sense to me."

"Sure it does; see, if them Navy boys pull into foreign ports and get punched-up by Army boys, then Navy boys retreat to their ships and nurse their wounds; this way there's no dixie-cups on the streets, so house-momma doesn't raise prices, so Army boys' dimes as good as gold. And that's a good thing for us back home, because it means Army boys, and Navy boys too, come home with more money in their pockets, so it'll cost Uncle Sam less money to float them GI Bills. That means there's a lesser need for the Government to borrow money, so naturally interest rates stay low so long as Government spending stays in check. Sheesh, everyone knows that. Hell, why else you think that Army-Navy game gets so heated each

year? It's 'cause half them boys in the stands got a score to settle; for all them overseas black eyes. Anyways, who wants to talk about this junk; let's talk about something positive. So what's that you was saying; Big Hank used to get in lotsa fights back in his Navy days? Huh; I wonder why?"

"I know what'chu thinkin', Eulie, and you wrong. Big Hank got into fights to make money; not 'cause he's inflationary."

"Oh no, not Big Hank; he's an angel. So I imagine he must've come home with a laundry bag filled with socks stuffed with money, huh?"

"Socks stuffed with money? Only things stuffed in Big Hank's socks were his big ol' feet; and maybe some overgrown toenails cuttin' holes in 'em."

"Huh," said Eulie, "So I wonder where all Big Hank's fightin' money gone? Oh, don't matter none. So tell me, Champ, where them old pretty postcards on the fridge from?"

Champ walked over to the refrigerator and lifted two magnets. She flipped over the old postcards and read their port stamps. She turned back to Eulie, smiling; except Champ's smile looked demonic, as she reached for the knife drawer. "Gots to go," yelled Eulie, as she turned and ran into the wall, before jumping up to her feet and racing out through the front door.

Chapter Seven

As Bunny rounded the corner she was met by a flat, dark cloud creeping towards her. It cast an ominous shadow over the entire park, including her duplex, which was only one city block away. From where she was, she could see her storm door open itself, and smack shut.

The sound of a knocking, gurgling car engine caught her attention. Not because it sounded like the car needed a tune-up, or because it popped the curb on its turn; but because someone had just cut its engine. The car slowly rolled-up alongside her. Bunny glanced over to see the car was actually a van; and it looked like the same old milk van from the food store parking lot. Most of the van's paint job had been stripped away, leaving a dull gray hue. It was similar in color to Champ's old aluminum pots.

From the passenger side, a man stepped out and walked towards Bunny. "How you doing this early evening, my friend?" he asked.

Bunny studied him. She didn't recognize him but something about him felt oddly familiar. He wore a flimsy blazer that stretched tightly across his shoulders. It appeared a size or two too small, as its sleeves rode up his forearms. It was dated and out of season; clearly too lightweight for today.

"What do you call yourself?" he asked. His voice had a slight lyrical cadence. He kept his head tilted to one side.

"What do I call myself?" asked Bunny, "What do you call yourself?"

"You my friend, you can call me… Jose."

"Right, well I don't have no money for you, Jose."

"Why do you think I want your money?" he asked, amused. "Do I look like I need your money?"

His tone was soft. He stepped closer. As he neared his eye color seemed to lighten. They had a golden-yellow tint as if someone shined a flashlight through a glass of ginger ale.

Bunny wasn't sure what a tiger's eyes looked like but she imagined they were similar. One thing she was certain of, there was no mistaking just how good-looking he was.

"I been watching you," he said, "I saw you back at the market."

His tone was even softer now, almost delicate. Bunny thought to herself, maybe people really do meet at the food store? Just then everything Champ ever drilled into her came flooding back. "Sorry, you're looking for a different kinda girl; it ain't me."

Jose turned-up his palms as if to show they were empty; something a magician might do before a trick. His hands quickly disappeared into his blazer's pockets. His resting arms now resembled chicken wings on account of how high his pockets were fastened on his ill-fitted blazer.

"What makes you think you ain't special?" he asked.

Bunny was taken aback, "Who said I ain't special? I know I'm special. Who are you anyways?"

Bunny moved to cross the street. Jose skipped-up a few steps to stay in front of her; but careful not to invade her space.

"Hey, hold on…why you leaving? What I meant is you seem special; like you *magically* special." Jose pulled a hand from his blazer's pocket and tossed a tiny cloud of glitter up into the air, before it sprinkled down between them.

"Cute," said Bunny, "How many times have you used that one today?"

Jose smiled at Bunny, just as the old milk van's driver's side window cracked open, "Gato, vamonos! Esta perra moreno no tiene mierda," said the voice inside.

"Gato, huh?" asked Bunny, "Why you lying about your name, Jose? Your boy just busted you."

"What are you talking about, why can't I be both?"

"I'll tell you why; because if you're Latino then I guess that makes me, who, Charo?"

"*WhatmakesyouthinkIain'tLATINO?!*"

"Because you're trying too hard," said Bunny, "It's like you're *tryingtosoundLATINO!*"

"Is that so?"

"It's true; you should've gone with Hispanic instead."

"Hispanic, huh? Interesting."

"No; you know what's interesting, Jose? I knew there was something about you, something that seemed familiar to me; but I couldn't put my finger on it. But I got it now; it's that pidgin you're hiding. I sniffed-out that little French hiccup you're trying to disguise. Plus, you're a little dark for them Latino boys. Even mixed Afro-Latino boys ain't as dark as you. Not to mention your Spanish is weak. You talk like you've got hot food in your mouth. That's what people sound like when they're trying to imitate Latinos."

"I...I don't even know how to respond."

"Don't; just know your first give-away was that little Creole-magic glitter gag."

"Wasn't no gag; you seem magically special. That's all I was saying."

"So then why me?" asked Bunny.

"Let me ask you a question; why you so insulted to be a pretty girl? Or are you just offended someone like me found the courage to come get at you?"

"Isn't that two questions?"

"You know what? I should've known. It's obvious you're outta my league. I don't know what I was thinking. I'll stop bothering you. My apologies, and thank you my friend."

"What are you thanking me for?" asked Bunny.

"Thank you for letting me down gently. You are most kind. Be well my friend." Jose turned and started walking back towards the old milk van.

Bunny wasn't sure why, or what, she was feeling guilty about, but she was. "Hey Jose, don't apologize. It's just that I have somewhere to be; that's all."

Jose stopped and turned around, "So then let me take you."

Bunny was taken aback, "Take who? Take me? Nuh-uh."

"Why not?" asked Jose, "Why does someone being kind to you seem so foreign?"

"Because I don't even know you."

"So what; one-night stands don't know each other, either."

"Okay…that was really creepy. This conversation is over." Bunny picked up her pace.

"No wait; I'm not sayin' we should do the hook-up."

Bunny stopped and looked at Jose, *"Do the hook-up?"*

"You make me nervous my friend; I'm not a good talker in front of pretty girls."

"I highly doubt that, Jose. You're a little too handsome to play the dopey/shy card."

"It's true, heartbreaker."

"Heartbreaker?"

"Yes; you break my heart. You won't even trust me to take you to wherever you need to go."

Bunny's eyebrows lifted, "You really thought I would just go ahead and jump inside that kidnap van with you?"

"Kidnap van? My friend, life is about choices; is it not? We must have the courage to take risks and leap forward. By not taking chances, do we not risk the most? Just think, marriages are chances, are they not? And I bet half of all marriages started with one-night stands, no?"

"I'm not having this discussion," said Bunny, "Not to mention, what was that anyways, some sort of bizarro marriage proposal?"

"It's only an observation of people my friend; and the chances people are willing to take so long as you call them something else."

"So, you talkin' from experience, Jose?"

"One-night stands?"

"No! Marriage. Let me see your ring finger."

"Me, married? Am I married? Hell no. Everyone says you know when you know, but I ain't one to know how to know when you know; know what I'm sayin'? Seems that whole part of life just passed me right by. Wasn't against it any; just that I ain't met that special person yet. But who knows, maybe this chance-meeting ain't so chance; like, maybe fate is sneaking in as we speak?"

"Que sera sera; huh? You dig Sly?" asked Bunny.

"I'm down with Mr. Stone; no doubt. But what do you say my friend, let me take you; it's about to pour."

"*No way Jose.* Ain't nothing personal but by rule I don't do the kidnap van thing; especially ones that I suspect probably have a mattress in the back. But let me ask you, what kind of friend are you?"

"How do you mean?"

"I mean, what kind of friend leaves their boy stuck in the kidnap van this long? You know he's probably breaking a sweat paging back and forth in his little English to Spanish dictionary, trying to decide what to shout out next."

"Wait; so you don't think my boy's *LATINO* either?"

"I love how hard and fast you say *LATINO*. As for whether he's *LATINO* or not, I don't know; but I've been around Latinos enough to tell you he don't sound Latino. His Spanish sounds more like 8th grade Español class. At best he's Mexican."

"Oh shit, I don't even know what that means? You a spicy one, huh? You sure you ain't Latina?"

"It means he doesn't sound Caribeño; that's all."

"I tell you what my friend, let me go ask my boy if we can give you a ride. Then I'll introduce you and you can decide on whether or not he's *LATINO;* or Mexican. Okay?"

"You ain't gotta introduce us; I already know who he is."

"You do? So who is he?"

"Well, if you're *Jose*, wouldn't that make him *Hose-B?*"

"You're so crazy! You always this fun? What's your name funny girl?"

"Bunny."

"Bunny? No way, like little soft bunny rabbit?"

"That's right, Spanish Joe."

The buzzing streetlight above flickered. Bunny and Jose both glanced up and watched it flicker again, before dying. Bunny looked back at Jose and busted him checking her out. She gave him a quick once-over and slow-played it, so he'd catch her.

"So what'chu think, Bunny?"

"Wait, so I ain't your friend no more?"

"Sorry; so what'chu think, Bunny, my friend?"

"What do I think? I think you better hurry up and get my phone number before it starts raining and I dust you."

"You'd do me like that?" asked Jose.

"Nah, I'm just playing, Jose. But the truth is what I told you already; I'm squeezed for time today but I *might* be interested in a rain check; assuming you got a pen and some scratch paper in the love bus."

Jose paused for a moment, as did Bunny, but Bunny's silence was her waiting for him to respond. With each passing moment it became harder and harder for her to fend off her insecurities. Prompting someone to take down her phone number was unchartered waters for her. The wait was killing her; she couldn't take it anymore, "So you gonna grab that pen, Jose...or is this it?"

Jose turned his head away for a second, like he was thinking; before turning back to Bunny, "So what, funny girl calling the shots now?"

Bunny sensed a slight change in his tone. The van's driver's side door opened. It was the same driver from the food store parking lot; the one that raised a fist at her. He approached and stood uncomfortably close. His tall frame towered over Bunny. He stared directly down on her, prompting Bunny to take one step back. He reached down into her grocery bag and pulled out a Granny Smith. He opened his mouth wide and smashed the apple against his teeth; like buckshot, tiny pieces of apple sprayed across Bunny's face.

"So, what's up?" he asked.

Bunny tried not to watch him grind the apple, but he chewed it with his mouth wide open.

"Bunny's in a hurry," said Jose.

"The tall one seemed confused. "Bunny? Conejo?"

Jose nodded.

"Huh, how you like that; *conejo negro*. So what'chu say hombre, you ready?"

"Yeah, I'm ready," said Jose, "But Bunny here thinks your Spanish sucks; like you got hot tamales in your mouth or some stupid shit. I think she's got problemas with los Mexicanos también. Hold up."

Headlights advanced on the park's entrance and stopped. An intense beam of light flipped-on from the vehicle's driver's side window, blinding all three of them. Jose turned towards Bunny with a big smile, "Hug me," he said.

"I ain't hugging you," scoffed Bunny.

Jose's high cheek bones flexed as he faked an even wider smile. Through clenched teeth, "I said, hug me bitch." Jose leaned forward and squeezed Bunny tight, crinkling the paper bag in-between them.

"Get your hands off me, or I'll scream," said Bunny.

The floodlight popped-off as the car at the park's entrance flipped on its cherries and pulled a U-turn before disappearing.

"Alright, you can chillax, Bunny. We good."

"You ain't from around here," said Bunny, "Where you from?"

Ain't No Sunshine

"So what, now you Inspector Cousteau?" asked Jose.

Bunny paused a second, "Here's how I know you're not from around here; if you were, you'd know all them cops are white; and white-boy cops don't come down dimly lit streets, at least not in Newark; not since the riots. Sure, if they're tipped off about some untraceable loot, then yeah, they're cowboys again; but for the most part they prefer to stick to car searches on the main roads. And that's so other white-boy cops can spot them quick, and provide show-of-force psych-ops; it's nothing new. Not to mention, that was a city cop and we're in a county park; meaning the two don't mix. So that's how I know you ain't from around here; 'cause you as locally street-dumb as you are with your movie inspectors."

Jose smiled at Bunny and then his eyes darted from her to the tall one, before shooting a quick glance at the van's back doors. The tall one took a fresh bite of the Granny Smith and with his other hand he pulled the old van's door lever, as both rear doors popped open, exposing an old stained mattress without a sheet. The sound startled Bunny, causing her to glance over her shoulder. Staring back at her was Lady Liberty, from the middle of the old milk van's white license plate.

"Put her bag in the van," said Jose.

The tall one seemed giddy as he lifted Bunny's grocery bag straight up out of her arms and placed it inside the van's back doors. "About time," said the tall one, "And I tell you what hombre; if it's true what they say, that time is money, then this was one shitty investment. Remind me to enroll you in some business classes when we get back."

A peppering of rain drops masqueraded Bunny's watery eyes. She felt like a fool. She snatched back her grocery bag.

"Easy, Bunny..." said Jose, "I want you to nicely hand your grocery bag back to the tall gentleman who is then going to place it back inside the van."

"Nuh-uh; ain't happening."

"Bunny, I'm trying to work with you, here."

"You're trying to work with me? Fuck you Jose; and fuck Hose-B, too."

The tall one looked confused, "Who the fuck is Hose-B? Am I Hose-B?" He turned and fired the Granny Smith at the stop sign. It exploded on impact; making a gong-like sound. "See that you fuckin' mutt; that'll be you." he said, "I don't play, you got that?"

"Chill, I got this," said Jose, calmly; before turning back to Bunny, "I'm sorry about that; it's been a long day. But this doesn't have to drag out any longer. I'm going to ask you again, nicely. Would you please hand your grocery bag back to the tall gentleman who will then place it inside the van?"

The tall one was visibly agitated. He grabbed Bunny's bag but she wouldn't let go. He clenched his teeth and leaned into her; pressing his fist against her cheek. Bunny turned and looked at Jose.

"Don't look at him, stupid," said the tall one, "He ain't gonna help you."

Bunny let go of the grocery bag as the tall one lifted it straight up from her arms and placed it inside the van. Jose could now see the tracks of Bunny's tears. He wanted this to end. Jose turned to the tall one and in a serious tone he was precise: "Inside the grocery bag is a small white purse. Take the purse out of Bunny's bag and place it under the mattress. Then hand the bag of groceries back to Bunny and let her be on her way. But before you do all that, I want you to apologize to Bunny, for pressing your fist on her. That wasn't cool; she didn't do anything to you."

"Apologize?" asked the tall one, with a slight grimace. He lowered his head until he and Bunny were eye to eye, "*Chupa mi polla gorda!*" He turned back to Jose, "How's that?"

"This is my game!" yelled Jose, "I'm the union boss. I'm the Mayor, the Governor, the Senator, all rolled into one. I know what's best for everyone, and I decide; that's how democracy works today. So do as I ask, please."

"Yo, you're trippin'," said the tall one, "We're wasting our time here. Who comes to Newark to roll people? She ain't no fuckin' drug dealer. You said there was some stoner house filled with dopey blanquitos that was ripe for the takin'; but instead we got us this dumb bitch who looks like she ate all the stoners' munchies. And what's she even got in that shitty

121

little thrift store purse anyway, two bucks? She ain't even worth the fuckin' tolls."

"Listen'up," said Jose, "You're my boy, but you're proving to be a liability, here. You need to do as I ask so we can pull-out; and Bunny can get on with going to wherever it is she needs to be going."

The blinking traffic light creaked as it rocked back and forth. Hammering raindrops pelted the roof of the old milk van. It was loud and rhythmically fast. Rainwater rushed along the curb. Bunny could feel her feet getting wet through her sneakers. She locked-in on Jose, and glared at him. The streetlight above unexpectedly flickered-on again. The light caught Jose by surprise, revealing his tilted-away side. Bunny could see he'd been shy about a birthmark. It was unusual; it had long, dark, wave-like markings that tattooed his entire tilted-away side.

Bunny's adrenaline was spiking. Jose turned his birthmark away but Bunny moved her head in front of his so they were face to face. "You sorry-ass lowlife," she said, "You crossed that river to rob some white-boy trustafarians of their dime bags, and when you couldn't figure out where they lived, you decided to roll me instead? You're a sad mutherfucker, you know that? No, I take that back; you're a pathetic mutherfucker; like I feel sorry for you. You're garbage."

"You finished?" asked Jose.

"No, I'm not finished. Here, take my money. It's not even in my purse; it's in my pocket." Bunny pulled out a small handful of bills and crunched them, before throwing them at Jose. A small ball of bills bounced off Jose's chest, and fell to the street. "Twenty-nine dollars, Jose, you scored. You're a real gangster. Now pick it up, PICK IT UP! Pick up my money, bitch."

Jose looked down at the wet bills on the street before looking up at Bunny, and grinning, "So you better than me now, *my friend?*"

"FUCK YOU!!!" screamed Bunny.

The tall one stepped between them and whispered to Jose, "What the fuck are we doing? Fuck this fat-titty bitch."

Jose peeked out from around the tall one, "Happy now Bunny? You're getting everyone upset. And just so you know it ain't polite to throw your money at people. If I was the thug you need me to be, I'd probably grab you by your neck and stick your face in that money, to teach you a lesson. But that ain't me; I treat everyone with respect that treats me with respect. See, I wasn't rude to you, was I? My partner now, well, he's different. He's what I call 'a wildcard.' So for the good of everyone, mostly you, you might want to break-out that apology right about now. See, us 'garbage' is willing to chalk this up as a misunderstanding. So what do you say, Bunny, you got an apology in you today?"

"You want me to apologize to you; for rolling me?"

"I didn't roll you; you threw your money at me."

"Uh-huh, well how's this for an apology, Jose: *Fuck you and your filthy whore mother.*"

"Ooh-hoo! Still spicy; you sure you ain't *LATINA?!*"

Bunny squint both eyes at Jose until his smile disappeared. His top lip stayed in place, hanging-up over a bulging incisor. His teeth suddenly looked too big for his mouth. For the first time Bunny noticed how chipped and jagged they were. She couldn't believe just moments ago she was taken by him.

"Why you looking at me like that, Bunny?" asked Jose, "Like you so disgusted by the sight of me?"

The tall one waved his hand in front of Jose's face, to get his attention, "Yo, it's time. Let's get outta here."

Jose smirked at the tall one, before nodding his head, "We good." Jose turned back to Bunny, who was still glaring at him. "I know this is going to disappoint you, Bunny, but I can't make you happy. See, I know how bad you need for me to pick-up that money. But I can't do it. If I pick up that money it buys you the lie that you're better than me."

"Hombre, vamonos."

"Chill, I'm coming," said Jose, before turning back to Bunny, "Just let me ask you this; you're a little bit lonely, right? Maybe underappreciated too? You ever get depressed, like life's less dreamy than you've imagined it; or maybe it's unfair at times? Now mix in how you're getting long in the tooth, or tight in the jeans, and you're just realizing now,

Ain't No Sunshine

Prince Charming and his fat wallet, well, he don't see you; he's at the go-go bar negotiating daddy-issue rates, in the Champagne Room. Sure, there's chunked-up, antique fellas looking for a diaper change; but then his adult children will dictate your suicide note, at gunpoint. So if things seem bleak, *believe it.*

Bunny's chest began to swell with each rapid, short breath.

"And that's why I get you, Bunny. You're assigning all that pain; all that reality to me, like I'm some sub-species of you. 'Cause if I'm lesser than you, then it gives you an artificial boost in supremacy. And you need that fake booster shot of self-confidence to hide how broken you are; before it consumes you. See, I'm protecting you from you. I'm the drum you need to beat on. So sure, I'll play the role of your creation; your *Ghetto Frankenstein,* but rather than you throw your money at me, hand it to me and say *mèsi.*

"Yo, I'm leaving," said the tall one, before walking back to the driver's side of the van.

"I'm coming," said Jose, before turning back to Bunny, "And before you go calling a person 'garbage,' just know I spotted you today because you looked ready. Like you're tired of what you got, or don't got going on. I recognize it 'cause I'm the same. And that's why I'd bet your twenty-nine dollars that you and I would've gotten-on famously."

A squiggly, pulsating vein throbbed thru Bunny's temple; her short breaths were even more rapid than before.

Jose's voice softened into a reminiscing-like tone, "Always loved me a girl with an off sense of humor; ain't easy to come by. Shit, I had us pegged for driving cross-country; laughing and joking, and asking strangers to take pictures of us in front of dumb shit, and doing all them things people do when they're jiving with one another. But if I'm gonna be honest, after a while I'd probably grow tired of you. Curiosity will have worn off and you'll sense it; and then you'll do what bitches do; you'll sleep with one of my boys, or pander to ghouls from your past to stuff that wrinkle; all because you need validating. Naturally, it'll send me on my way, but you'll be relieved because now you'll have me to hate on. I'll be the crutch that keeps you from hating you."

Bunny's breathing was laborious; she closed both eyes and began rocking in place.

"So, if you were me Bunny, meaning I was you, and I took a hard look in the mirror, I wouldn't be happy, neither. Truth is, no one likes their reflection once they see they're just another uppity, racist white bitch trapped inside a fat black ghetto girl. Now give up that fuckin' pea coat."

Bunny lunged at Jose, ripping into his face and dragging her nails deeply across his pretty side. The tall one came running from the side and blasted Bunny in the ear; the impact, like an explosion, knocked her clean off her feet. She landed hard in the street; her head ricocheting off the curb.

Ain't No Sunshine

Bunny lay motionless; her arms extended up in the air, stiff and frozen-like; her hand still curled like a bloodied claw. Her eyes came back to life and began blinking wildly, trying to cure her double vision. Her head rested against the curb awkwardly, before a thin stream of blood spilled from one nostril, and dripped from the other, as a clear fluid poured from one ear.

Swelling street water gushed up against her before finding its way around. Despite not being able to focus, Bunny could make out the gashes she left across Jose's pretty side; and how they mirrored the wavy stripes of his birthmark, on his dark side.

The streetlight above fizzled-out and died again, causing the corner's blinking traffic light to cast an eerie strobe effect into the night. With each blink, a scarlet hue cast against Jose's face. Bloodied and wild-eyed, he resembled a wounded tiger angrily pacing back and forth, back and forth.

Bunny's eyes tightened from the strain of tracking Jose's movements until she felt a pop, and blood-laced fireworks exploded through the whites of her eyes. She tried to lift herself out of the rising street water, but her limbs felt dead. She gargled for air as street water poured into her mouth; her unhinged jaw hung agape. Jose stepped closer. The ringing in her ears was halted by a primitive roar. Jose's cheekbones flexed as his teeth clenched. Bunny watched a sole ascend before thinking of her storm door, and wincing.

Chapter Eight

The tall one hoisted Bunny halfway up on to the floor of the van. He grabbed both of her legs like a wheelbarrow; first lifting them up and then dumping her over on to the old stained mattress. He adjusted her slightly, and pushed her head to the side, before slamming shut the back doors. With a bounce in his step, the tall one skipped towards the driver's side door and jumped-in.

"Guess that explains why you ain't never seen no black rabbit's foot on no key chain; ain't so lucky."

Jose wasn't amused.

"Yo! Wake up," said the tall one.

Jose turned and faced him, to prove he wasn't sleeping.

"Oh shit, she fucked you up good. That shit looks deep. You better hope you don't bubble-scar."

Jose turned away and cranked-up his window until it was sealed shut. He tucked his hand into his too short cuff and wiped away the rainwater on the door's interior.

The tall one looked over, "Yo, before you zone-out again, get me outta here. Jersey gives me the fuckin' creeps. Get me to my Welcome Back Kotter sign."

Jose dipped his head and looked through the dots of rainwater on his side-view mirror, "Hook a U-turn right here," he said, "Just watch-out for the lil'dawg with the jug, chasing the cart."

The tall one pulled a U-turn before flexing his hand while holding his wrist, "That bitch hurt my hand," he said, as he guided the steering wheel with his knee. The van slowed to a roll, and pulled over.

"What are you doing?" asked Jose.

The tall one climbed into the back; his big feet clumsily banging into everything. "You drive for a while…" he said.

Jose moved into the driver's seat, adjusted the rear view mirror and began to drive. He turned up the radio.

"Yo! Turn that shit down," said the tall one, "Let me concentrate."

Jose turned up the volume louder, and followed signs for the Pulaski Skyway. A few minutes later the tall one climbed back up front and bounced into the passenger seat. He was wetter than before and was now fidgeting with something.

"Who does this?" he asked, frustrated. "I need a scissors; never mind, I got it. Here…"

Jose pretended not to hear him, as the van's old single wiper smeared rainwater across the windshield.

"Yo, here…"

"You see I'm driving, right?" said Jose, aggravated. He leaned forward while looking up through the blurry windshield, trying to read highway signs as he drove underneath them.

"Chill hombre," said the tall one, "It's just a little rooster."

"It's Good Friday," said Jose, somberly.

The tall one slid the whole rooster into his mouth, "It's only marshmallow; doesn't count."

Jose pushed between the AM radio preset buttons. He was agitated that no signal was coming in besides jazz.

"Yo, leave that," said the tall one, "You hear that?"

Jose didn't feel like talking.

"Ya'know, I think that bitch clawed-out your eardrum. First you turn up that music like you're some old man hard of hearing, then you pretend like you don't hear me; or I ain't

131

worthy of no reply. If I didn't know better, I'd think you're ignoring me. So let me ask you this again, do you know what this is, like what's this type of music called?"

"Yeah, I know what it is," grumbled Jose.

"So then what's it called?"

"It's called 'some old bitch mumbling jazzy nonsense.'"

"Close; it's called *scatting*. It's an art; you feel it, interpret it, and let it fly. Whoever this bitch is, she's legit."

Jose interrupted him by pushing all of the radio presets hastily. Static, it was all static. He snapped off the radio.

"Yo, I was listening to that," said the tall one, before pulling out a cigarette and sniffing it. "Shit smells old; like dead people." He lit the cigarette and sucked in a big deep drag before coughing like he was down a lung.

Jose looked over at him, amazed.

"What?" asked the tall one, in-between coughs.

"Who told you it was cool to light up in here?"

"You serious? Man, you're moody," said the tall one, "What's got you so pissy?" The tall one cranked-down the passenger window just enough to flick-out the old cigarette. "Menthol is so fuckin' nasty," he said, "I don't know how anyone smokes that shit." He rolled down the window a hair more, and dropped-out the entire pack. A windy rain pinned the cigarette pack to the window; its cellophane wrapper created a suction-like seal against the wet glass.

Ain't No Sunshine

"Who the fuck is that?" asked the tall one, before delivering a quick backhand to the glass, trying to knock the pack loose from the window. Outside looking in was Big Hank; his image slid down the wet glass in a seesaw fashion before coming to a rest along the bottom ledge of the window.

The tall one turned the radio back on and pushed all the presets until he found the jazz station again, and smiled at Jose. In whipsaw fashion, the tall one snapped his head sideways and looked out the side window, "Yo!" he said, "Did you see that? It said '*Ode to Flannery*' with peacocks and shit. It's a fuckin' peacock farm, yo; some kinda fucked-up Jersey garden with peacocks and shit. Let's go snatch us a peacock, I'll cook that bitch."

"Peacocks are bucks," said Jose, matter-of-factly, "Peahens are bitches."

The tall one thought about it for a second, "Whatever; turn us around and I'll cocknap one, you watch."

Jose ignored him and instead attacked the radio presets until he found a clear signal that wasn't jazz.

As the old milk van crossed the Pulaski, Big Hank's cigarette pack began to flicker against the wind before finally detaching from the wet window and fluttering away; sailing down into the Hackensack.

The tall one sensed he was being ignored again, so he pushed a random radio preset button. He guessed right, as the old lady was still scatting. He turned up the volume and smiled at Jose, waiting for his reaction.

"Your brain hard of oxygen?" asked Jose.

"What's that?"

"You heard me," said Jose, before clearing his throat. "Sad part is you don't even know what you just done."

"So what'd I do?" asked the tall one.

"You just changed Bill Withers, mutherfucker; that's what you just done."

"Yo, that was messed up," said the tall one, "Don't talk to me like I'm some bitch; this is *my* van."

The old milk van jolted hard from taking-on a Jersey-size pothole; its impact launched a hubcap high into the air and over the skyway's iron railing. The old van continued chugging along as it climbed a jug-handle ramp. As it circled around, the old van came face to face with a mountainous panorama of skyline. Lights, small pockets of darkness, and the illuminated backside of Lady Liberty, all of them smeared together into a single blur across the wet windshield.

Jose dropped the old van into neutral, and they coasted down the ramp and into an idle brigade of red brake lights. As the old van rolled to a stop, cars quickly filled in on all sides of them. Straight ahead, between wet wiper smears, Jose and the tall one watched cars funnel in, one by one, into the tunnel below the Hudson; just beyond an unexpected, random DUI check-point at the tunnel's entrance.

Ain't No Sunshine

Through a constant chorus of honking horns, Bunny's hearing slowly came back. She could hear "The Divine One" mixed with the sound of rain; it must be Easter, she thought. Surprisingly she felt good...cool. She smelled fresh, wild mint.

The End